Theft at the Speed of Light

By Michael Galloway

ISBN-13: 978-0-9847402-1-5

www.michaelgalloway.net

This is a work of fiction. Names, characters, places, and events are products of the author's imagination or are used fictitiously. Any resemblance to actual persons, living or dead, locations or events is entirely coincidental.

Scripture taken from the HOLY BIBLE, NEW INTERNATIONAL VERSION, Copyright © 1973, 1978, 1984 International Bible Society. Used by permission of Zondervan Bible Publishers.

Chapter One

At high noon, thousands of checking accounts across America went empty. According to the radio, it first began as a series of scattered bank server outages. It was later discovered to be a series of rapid-fire electronic withdrawals of unknown origin, followed by crippling denial-of-service attacks against several banking websites. An hour later, dozens of customers at a bank in Manhattan, Kansas, were informed their credit had been trashed. An hour after that, several retirees in Plant City, Florida, found their savings accounts plundered and their IRAs looted.

Alex Poole clicked off the news reports of the thefts on the car radio and pulled off the interstate. He then drove up next to a gas pump at Adam's Pit Stop and Convenience Store near his workplace in Woodbury. The Pit Stop was a combination of a repair garage, convenience store and gas station, decorated inside and out with a black and white checkerboard pattern and cherry red trim. Out in the front parking lot, they even had a red-and-white Formula One racer on display, along with a food stand selling hot dogs and soft drinks.

He climbed out of his car and was met with a wall of heat and humidity that must have broken a record somewhere. The bank thermometer across the street only read ninety-two in the shade. It was not long before the hazy, mid-August Minnesota sun caused beads of sweat to form on his forehead.

He walked around his car to the pump, selected the blue "pay inside" button and lifted the nozzle. As soon as the pump was authorized, he unscrewed his fuel cap and began to fill the tank. In seconds, the odor of gasoline struck him full force and threatened to knock him off balance. Surely this heat would make for great thunderstorms later on and sure enough, off to the west, he noticed black clouds roiling on the horizon.

Against the storm front, his eyes locked onto a new freeway

billboard just down the street. The slogan across the top of the billboard read "Liberty Cards. Safe. Secure. Superior." Underneath that a woman with magnetic eyes proudly held up a snazzy royal blue Aspirizon Bank card in her palm of her hand. With raven hair, ruby lips, and Halloween a mere two months away, he half expected sparks to be flying from her fingertips.

He shook his head and smirked.

The pump thumped to a stop. He returned the nozzle to its holder and replaced the fuel cap. Like a determined athlete, he plowed his way through the humidity until he reached the front door of the store.

Once inside, he veered to the left and snatched an icy lemonade from a refrigerator case in the back. Condensation was forming on the cases, however, and it felt like the cooling system in the building failed hours earlier. From a wire rack near the front door, he grabbed a newspaper and approached the counter.

In front of him, a young Chinese man in his early twenties paid for a pack of Marlboros, red box. To his left he noticed a rust-stained door that read "Repair Garage" and to the left of that on the wall were a series of black and white explosion diagrams showing the insides of a car's suspension and a transmission. Beneath those were a pair of empty booths with tables. On one of the tables he spotted what appeared to be an abandoned black Toshiba Satellite laptop, much like the one he owned at home.

He stared at it a moment until the cashier's voice broke his concentration.

"Sir?" The cashier said.

"Sorry. Say, it looks like someone left their laptop behind over there."

Alex turned towards the counter and set his newspaper and lemonade on the counter. "Gas on pump four," he said, pointing back towards his car.

The cashier scanned the items on the counter. Alex then held out his bank debit card to the cashier.

The cashier was a gruff, rosy-cheeked man in his mid-thirties, with concrete mixers for arms, and black, slicked back hair. His gray mechanics coveralls barely fit his frame. He swiped the card and punched out the dollar amount on a keyboard covered with some type of protective plastic. In the background, a dusty gray fan swung back and forth, rustling papers on the counter.

"This card is no good," the cashier said in a deep baritone voice, still holding the card in his hand.

"What do you mean it's no good?"

"Bank's declining it."

"Are you sure you didn't swipe it too fast?"

"I said it's no good."

"Sometimes a plastic bag over the card works, too."

The cashier then put his palms down on the counter and gave Alex a vacant stare. "I'll bet it does." He then tossed the card onto the counter. "You got anything else, buddy?"

Alex spotted engine grease on the man's hands. Puzzled, he picked up the card, checked it for grease marks, and slid it back into his wallet. "Here, try this one."

"If you need money, I'm sure somebody at the mission down the street could help ya," said a woman behind him.

He glanced back to see a woman in her late fifties fanning herself with a newspaper. With curly white hair and flipped-up sunglasses, she looked sour enough to make his lemonade seem like bottled water.

"I have the money. My card isn't working."

He turned back toward the cashier, and heard a muzzled "mmmph" from the woman as if to fire off one last verbal mortar round. Again, he watched the cashier slide the card through the reader, punch in the dollar amount, and wait. He practically counted every pack of cigarettes behind the mechanic-turned-cashier's head before the register printer buzzed out a receipt.

"You're lucky," the man said.

Alex signed his name and slid the receipt back. He watched the cashier hold up the signed receipt next to the back of the card to compare signatures and then slide the card and a copy of the receipt back to Alex. He crammed both items into his wallet and heaved a sigh of relief.

As he exited the store, he pulled out his cell phone and dialed the bank. He sped through the automated menus to reach his checking account balance. Today was payday, and by his estimation, he should have plenty of money left in his account.

Or so he thought.

"Negative thirteen dollars and twelve cents," the machine read back in a mechanical female voice.

He thumbed the translucent buttons on his phone to check the transaction history. Four checks cleared days ago, all with out-of-sequence numbers, all with amounts in the hundreds of dollars. Having no pen, paper or patience, he slipped back into his car and slammed the door. He started the engine and punched his black Buick Century into reverse to pull away from the pumps.

Where were the checks cashed? Was anybody still writing checks? And most important, how did they get the information in the first place?

On the seat next to him, he flipped open his checkbook and glanced at the ledger at the next red light. The last entry in the checkbook was from the weekend.

He decided that the next step would be to shut the account down, and shut it down fast. That is, if the bank cooperated first.

Chapter Two

For twenty minutes, Alex drove home in volcanic silence. He left the radio off and instead studied the ashen storm clouds looming overhead. Lightning flickered in the distance while the trees stood eerily still.

In his neighborhood, he passed the usual two-story homes, an apartment complex and a handful of townhomes. Today, though, they seemed dwarfed by the events in the sky. He pulled down his home street and into the driveway of his tan, split-level townhome with a two-car garage. At the foot of the driveway he clicked the garage door opener and noticed Danielle's car in the left stall. In the front yard he saw a newly stuffed black lawn bag sitting next to her yellow, orange and crimson marigold flower bed. Her sunburst design was always a reassuring splash of color on an otherwise drab day.

Once inside the house, he bounded up the carpeted stairs leading from the garage up to the living room. From there, he went straight ahead into the kitchen and grabbed the cordless phone off the charger. He noticed three freshly picked zucchinis on the counter, too, along with two fresh cucumbers and a pile of leaf lettuce. On the way back out into the hallway and into his bedroom, he dodged his son's abandoned toy fire truck in the middle of the floor.

Thunder rumbled as he strode into the master bedroom and closed the door behind him. On his nightstand he flipped on the light, but it flickered a moment. He kept waiting in anticipation for the power to fail, but as soon as the flickering stopped, he dialed the bank. He sped through the automated menus yet again until he reached a live person.

"CamdenBank, this is Rebecca. How can I help you?" The representative said in a drawl straight out of South Georgia.

"Somebody's writing checks against my account. I need to close it down."

"Okay, sir. For verification purposes, what is your mother's maiden name?"

"Payne."

"Thank you."

"Now, there are four checks that cleared last Friday. Numbers 504, 3817..."

"Okay, one moment. I see those."

"Great. Now, I don't write out checks for anything but bills. Things like the mortgage, the electric bill..."

"You didn't use any out of sequence checks by any chance, did you? Like from another box, or did you buy some checks through a third party? Many customers do that."

"No. I only order them through you, and I'm currently on check number 2587."

"Sir, do you have any automatic payments coming out of your account?"

"No."

Alex sat down on the edge of the bed and scribbled notes. Despite the light on the nightstand, the shadows in the room seemed to grow longer by the minute. Again, the lights flickered a moment.

"Have you let anybody else use your checkbook lately?" She asked.

"Wow. No. My wife has her own account. Listen, those checks aren't mine."

"Sir, we do offer the ability to look at cashed checks online. Have you tried that?"

"I don't bank online."

"Sir, it's easy and convenient. You just go to our website..."

"I get all that. Can you mail them out to me instead?"

"Do you have a problem with our website?"

"Lady, I'm a software engineer. I don't have problems with your website."

"Okay," she replied after a few seconds of typing. Then she started to pop bubbles with her chewing gum.

"And then what?" He said impatiently.

"I can have an affidavit of forgery mailed to you or you can stop into a branch to pick up one at the customer service desk."

"How can I close my account then?"

"Darlin', you have to do that at a branch. Or do you have problems with that too?"

He threw a hand up in the air. "Wait. What if more checks come out between now and then?"

"Those will be your responsibility."

"My responsibility?"

"That's right. Now, as a one-time courtesy to you, I can have these charges reversed, along with the associated fees provided you send us the proper documentation. May I place you on hold a minute?"

"Wait. What? A one-time courtesy? You guys let my..."

The line went silent. He put the earpiece of the telephone against his forehead. The curtains in the bedroom seemed to get darker as the call dragged on. In a minute, the representative came back on the line.

Before she could even speak, Alex took the initiative. "Okay, let me get this straight. If my account gets hit again, it's suddenly *my fault?*"

"Well, darlin', if you close your account then those fees would not apply, but the account would be subject to a closing fee."

He ran his hand through his short, black hair and threw himself backwards onto his pillow. "So the worst case scenario would be that I would get hit again, pay fees for checks I never wrote, and pay another fee to close it all out?"

"That's right, darlin'."

"Okay. I'm done with you guys."

"Excuse..."

He hung up. The faster his mind raced, the slower the behemoth corporate bank bureaucracy seemed to move. What frustrated him, though, was that he had gone to great lengths for years to protect his personal information by signing privacy agreements and notices, and shying away from checks when he could. Yet through all his defenses, both technological and simple, nothing held and he felt himself laying there helplessly on the bed.

Then came a quiet knock at the door.

"Come in," he groaned.

Danielle, his wife, opened the door. She stood in the doorway sporting a muddied, yellow State Fair tee shirt and worn-out work jeans. Her wavy, shoulder length brown hair was trapped in a ponytail beneath her wide-brimmed canary yellow sun hat. "Everything okay?"

For a moment, he gazed into her eyes. They reminded him of inset smoky quartz. "My bank account was hit."

"No."

"Yes. Somebody wrote bad checks against it. I went to use my card at the gas station and they declined it. Come to find out four checks were drawn against my account and none of them were mine. The bank is sending me copies of the checks in the mail when they get a hold of them."

"Did you have enough for gas?"

"I had my other card."

A smirk crossed her face. She put one hand on her hip and pointed a dirty garden spade at him. "Good. Because you know what they say. If you drove off without paying, it could cost you your license."

"I'm being serious. Here, look at this." He held out his checkbook and his notes for her to read.

She grabbed them and bounced herself onto the edge of the bed. "Looks to me like you are writing secret checks. Alex, if there is anything you want to tell me now to clear the air…"

He sighed, but tried to deliver the news in a deadpan voice. "I do. I confess I have a secret life. I drained our vacation fund and cornered the market on Sour Patch Kids. I admit, I'm an addict. Seriously, though, what the heck? I'm switching to your bank tomorrow."

Thunder rumbled again as raindrops slapped at the bedroom window. He stood up to leave the room, but she reached up to touch his shoulder. "Sit down and tell me more first."

As he elaborated on what else he knew, Danielle began to knead his shoulders with her hands. He allowed her hands to steal away his anger if only for the afternoon. It was the best kind of theft he could think of.

Chapter Three

A steady rain was falling the next afternoon when Alex arrived at the CamdenBank branch near his home. From the road, the building looked like a two-story, brown brick castle with pine green awnings. The landscape around the exterior, however, was overrun with weeds. In addition, a row of untamed bushes near the front door appeared destined to fend for themselves.

He tucked his checkbook into his black windbreaker and ducked out of his car. From this distance, it looked as if the branch closed early, since there did not seem to be many lights on inside. He checked his watch, and then squinted to read the hours posted on the lobby door. He still had half an hour.

He dodged a five foot puddle near the door and stepped inside. In the airlock, he was struck with a musty smell that intensified in the main lobby. Against the far wall he spied a water stain running from floor to ceiling, along with some bulging wallpaper. In the background, he heard the steady sound of water dripping into a bucket. The roof of this fortress apparently had seen better days.

Alex walked in between the rope partitions in front of the counter, although no one stood in line before him. In fact, the lobby seemed unusually empty compared to the last time he visited.

The only open teller window was staffed by a woman whose nametag read "Robin". She looked out now at the lobby with tired eyes, even though she looked to be in early twenties. She brushed back a lock of her straight, auburn hair and put on a warm smile.

"Can I help you?"

Alex approached the counter, steeling himself for a confrontation. "Hi. I'd like to close my account."

Her smile disappeared in an instant. "You and everyone else."

He drew back a moment before placing his driver's license and his checkbook onto the green marble counter. The marble was trimmed with tarnished brass in desperate need of a cleaning and a bottle of polish.

"Sorry. It's been a long day," Robin said.

"You're telling me."

"Do you have your account number?"

He opened up his checkbook and turned it towards her. "I need an affidavit of forgery, too."

Robin sighed and withdrew a folded form from beneath the counter. She turned to her right and looked towards a doorway which lead to a back office of some sort. She brushed back her long auburn hair with her right hand and leaned forward to whisper, "I can't tell you how many of these I've pulled out today."

"Have you found out who's doing this?"

She shrugged her shoulders.

"Maybe you guys should hire some real investigators," he said.

"Know any? This is turning into a silent run."

"What's that?"

She leaned forward again and whispered. "When lots of people pull their money, but it doesn't make the news."

She picked up a form off the printer behind the counter. She slid it forward for him to sign. Near the bottom of the form, the balance read $1,237.53. He signed off on it as the only sound that could be heard in the bank was some shuffling papers at a desk behind him, and the steady drip, drip, drip of water in the corner. For a moment, the lights flickered and dimmed, then came back up to full intensity.

Robin swore under her breath as she clicked repeatedly at a couple of keys on her keyboard. She then slapped her mouse onto its mouse pad, as if it would help.

Alex slid the paperwork back.

She slammed the mouse down again and then reached down and restarted her computer. "Sorry. It will only be a minute."

Alex watched as her monitor went blank a moment and then came back to life. "Reboot?"

"You know it. Fun, huh?" She opened her drawer and began to count out the bills to Alex by the hundred. As she doled out the smaller bills and then the change, he felt the unprecedented urge to leave her a tip out of sympathy. Instead, he collected his money and his affidavit and headed for the front door. On the way out he dodged a gray, plastic bucket catching raindrops.

* * *

Alex drove across town to an Aspirizon bank branch near the Rosedale Mall in Roseville. This particular branch was a one-story building with a slanted, black, grooved roof and a drive-thru that made it look like a converted fast food restaurant. The smoked glass windows gave no hint of activity inside, but the crushed blue-gray rock around the perimeter appeared to be well-maintained, or maybe it was just low maintenance. The rain also seemed to lighten up a bit now, as the dank, low-hanging battleship-gray clouds steamed on towards the east. To the west, a clearing line even emerged.

He parked in the bank lot and climbed out of his car, surveying the surroundings as he went. He counted three cars in the parking lot and one pickup truck with a twenty year old man sorting through some paperwork. In the back of his truck were packs of shingles, several white five-gallon buckets, and a ladder. Alex stuffed his hands into his pockets as his eyes darted back and forth in front of him. It was not everyday that he walked around in public with several hundred dollars in his pocket.

The interior of the bank stood in sharp contrast to the outdoors, and even to his old bank's lobby. The teller windows were made of white Formica with black Formica beneath waist level, with white tiles for flooring. Here, several people waited in a neat line inside black velvet ropes strung between polished brass stands. Two tellers worked the windows effortlessly. To his left, the bankers' desks were separated by wooden walls topped with glass window pane dividers, giving the whole place an open, almost space age feel.

Alex took his place in line, still examining his surroundings, and looking for signs of trustworthiness. In front of one teller window, a black and gold plastic sign touted the benefits of FDIC insurance. Across the top of the wall behind the tellers he spied a banner that echoed the billboard slogan he saw yesterday. He also counted four silver tube cameras above the banner pointing back in his general direction. In the corners were round mirrors.

When his turn in line came, he spoke up. "Hi...I need to open a new account."

The teller, a Japanese woman in her early twenties, smiled brightly. "Great. If you take a seat at an open banker's desk back there they will assist you."

Alex nodded and smiled and paced over to the first open desk, where a young woman with dishwater blonde hair in a ponytail sat down moments before.

"Afternoon," she said. "Can I help you?"

"I need to set up a new account."

"You came to the right place. Have a seat."

She directed him to a plush cobalt chair opposite her desk. A bundle of pink balloons were tethered to the coat hook behind and to the left of her chair began to sway back and forth. At the same time, the odor of fresh popcorn assaulted his senses as he heard a popcorn machine in the background start up.

"I should have introduced myself. Name's Amber," she said, extending a hand. Her nails were painted black and in that moment, he also noticed a subtle streak of blue running through her hair. She wore a black turtleneck sweater with minimal makeup. "So what type of account were you looking to open?"

"Checking. My other account got hit."

"Ouch." She typed something at her keyboard and stared at her screen. "Lots of that going on, I hear."

"Have they figured out who's behind it?"

"I'm not sure. I heard something about stolen laptops the other day. Lots of them, in fact."

Alex immediately thought of Adam's Pit Stop and sat up straighter in his chair.

She glanced at him and scrunched her eyebrows together a moment. "Oh, don't worry, Mr..."

"Poole. Alex Poole."

"Your money is safe with us, Mr. Poole."

"I sure hope so. My wife banks here."

"Oh great. Were you looking for a joint account?"

"No. Separate for now." He relaxed a bit as she withdrew a brochure from her desk and slid it toward him.

"Does your wife have one of these?" She said.

He looked over the brochure. Across the bottom it read: "Liberty Cards. Safe. Secure. Superior." Above that there was a picture of the

Statue of Liberty.

"No," he said after a moment of hesitation. "At least not yet."

"Here take another brochure for her. She'll love it once she reads about all the features." She tapped away at her keyboard for a few moments. Then: "Before we get started, could I see some identification?"

He withdrew his driver's license from his wallet. Then he pulled out his bundle of hundred dollar bills and set it before her.

Her eyes widened. "That's definitely enough to open an account."

Just as the popcorn machine stopped a group of voices from the airlock between the lobby and the parking lot erupted in laughter. Alex turned to see a group of executives in blue and black suits enter the lobby. One executive at the back of the group of four men and two women seemed especially upbeat. The executive waved to the tellers one by one and then waved in Amber's direction. Amber smiled and waved back.

The man stood about six feet tall, with black, swept back hair, bushy eyebrows and a blue pinstripe dress shirt under his suit coat. His patterned crimson tie clashed in the worst possible way with the rest of his outfit. Then he pointed and smiled at Alex.

Alex spun back around to stare at the desk but it was too late. Seconds later he felt a firm hand on his shoulder. Amber began to fidget with a pen at her desk.

"Is that you Alex?" Came a smooth, deep voice from behind him.

"Oh, it's me. How are you?"

"Doing great, buddy. Couldn't be better. Amber, you see to it here that my friend gets the VIP treatment."

Alex smiled uncomfortably and shook his hand.

"Good to see you again," the executive said. He turned back to his colleagues and returned to what looked like a tour of the place.

Amber leaned forward, still fidgeting with her pen, and whispered, "You know him?"

"Oh yeah. That's my old boss. We worked together in operations many years ago."

She slid a pink form across the desk for him to sign. "Did you know he's president now?"

Alex drew back. He put a hand back on his stack of bills on her desk as if to rethink things. "The president? Of this place?"

"Yes. You look nervous."

"It's just…"

"Oh, that lawsuit in the news a ways back? Whatta joke that was. Mr. Malloy gives tons of money every year to the arts. He's really big on helping the local theaters, too."

"I'm sure he is. He's quite the actor, too."

Amber gushed. "He was an actor?"

"Maybe I shouldn't have said that. He was a better musician than an actor."

He turned back to watch the executives head into a back office of some sort.

"Mr. Poole? Are you going to sign this?"

He turned to see her pushing the paperwork at him with her black nails. Something made him uneasy inside. After staring at the paperwork a moment, he rubbed his burning eyes.

He looked up at her. For a moment, he thought, if she just dyed her hair black and put on some bold lipstick, maybe sparks would fly from her fingertips—just like the billboard he had seen the other day.

Alex blinked and picked up a pen from her desk.

"You okay?" She said.

"I'm…I'm fine."

He reviewed the form, scanned over some legalese at the bottom, and signed the signature line. He watched her turn the paperwork back towards herself and then tear the copies apart.

Amber opened up her desk drawer and pulled out a navy blue checkbook cover and slid it across the desk to him. "This is your starter book of checks."

Alex picked up the checkbook and flipped through it.

"Was there anything else?" She said, sliding the paperwork back across to him.

"This is good. Thanks."

He stood up to leave.

"Hope you find out what happened to your other account."

"Oh, I'll find out. Believe me, I'll find out who did it."

Chapter Four

The windowless conference room at Hoyle-Aspen was dark until Alex flipped on the light switch. The room was for the most part featureless, with brown, hatched wallpaper and plum carpeting. To his right, a large, empty whiteboard with markers awaited new designs. In the middle of the room was a long, rectangular, wooden table surrounded by six plush vermilion chairs.

He walked around to the front of the table and set his laptop down. He then ran a pair of cables from his laptop into the side ports of the large screen, high-definition television in the front of the room.

Moments later, Alex was followed by his boss, Drew Arthur, who was the current owner of the company. He was a quiet man in his late fifties with short, receding gray hair, glasses and a salt-and-pepper colored beard. Alex always thought of him as a man in constant motion, and even as he sat down next to Alex, he looked as if he would spring up from the table a minute later and run laps around the room. As usual, Drew was wearing his typical combination of white tennis shoes and a gray business suit.

Drew was followed by the lead salesperson for the company, Charles Lantham. Charles was ex-high school star hockey player in his mid-twenties, with short brown hair, blue eyes and a sarcastic smile. Standing five-foot-six, he carried a manila folder under his arm and wore a crisp, dark blue dress shirt, a burgundy tie and a black business suit.

Next, Tom Caldwell, a towering sheriff from Walworth County in neighboring Wisconsin, entered the room dressed in a brown uniform. Rumored to be over six-foot-five, he was a former collegiate basketball player with jet-black, spiked hair and a strong, sharp jaw line. He joked easily with Charles about the state of professional basketball in Minnesota. Both men sat down across from Drew as Alex fired up the television and brought up his first PowerPoint slide on the screen.

The sheriff waved to Drew. To Alex this was a great sign. Sheriff Caldwell's jail had been struck by a recent series of odd, often embarrassing escapes that included visitors getting access via fake identification badges, civilian clothes being smuggled to inmates, and general lapses in monitoring.

"Good afternoon, gentlemen," Alex said, turning from the first slide towards the audience. "My name is Alex Poole, of course, and I'm the lead software engineer here at Hoyle-Aspen and also one of the co-leads on the Pegasus Project."

The first slide showed a white, clip-art picture of the mythical Pegasus on the company's midnight blue colored background. The left front hoof was in midair, while the other smashed into the ground, with white ones and zeroes flowing out of it.

He flipped to the next slide, which showed an aerial shot of the Minnesota Correctional Facility in St. Cloud. "As you know, modern prison security comes in a variety of forms. In many systems nowadays, advances in technology can be found everywhere, and thankfully your own prison system is no exception. But like every system there are gaps, and of course certain inmates will sometimes spend weeks if not months planning elaborate escape plans. Fortunately, these cases are still few and far between, but time is no longer on our side."

He then flipped to a slide showing a security camera in the corner of an inmate gymnasium. The camera peered down on the empty floor and appeared to be immobile. "These gaps, both physical and in terms of data, are being exploited in greater numbers. For instance, cameras can only cover so much floor space, and like it or not, even round-the-clock monitoring is far from perfect."

Alex looked back to see Charles' reaction. He tapped his clicker and brought up a slide of the Pegasus prototype ring. "In response, over the past two years we've developed the Pegasus system. This version, for instance, is a steel and titanium ring that fits around a prisoner's ankle. It keeps track of an inmate's location at all times, and in some cases can be helpful in discerning their activities."

A picture of a prison cell block came up next, with graphical, red box outlines every few feet along the wall, along with arrows pointing to them. "The rings continually transmit unique data to nearby sensors in the prison walls, and if an inmate should flee, it then triggers a silent alarm."

He then changed to a slide showing a close-up of a wall sensor, which looked like a small metal plate the size of a playing card. "Within the year, we'll have added GPS tracking capability, which opens up many new possibilities."

Alex turned to see Charles whispering something to the sheriff, who nodded. Charles then gazed straight ahead, smug as ever. "Right now," he continued, "we have achieved tracking ranges of up to a mile if the bracelets are taken off the premises."

Alex flipped through some schematics of the sensors themselves, and some statistics from two facilities in Arizona where an earlier version of Pegasus had been installed. One of the last slides was that of the database interface, which he was especially familiar with. On the screenshot of one of the behind-the-scenes database tables, he reread the titles of the fields to himself. Full name, aliases, a photograph file pointer, nationality, fingerprint information...

"Alex, hey, I have a question. It's a little off topic, but how many people do you think we could track with Pegasus?" Charles said.

"It depends on the receivers in the walls. From there, it's a matter of pushing the data through to the main server and into the database backend." He paused a moment as Drew and the sheriff continued discussing something. "Why?"

"We're looking at larger prisons down the road."

Sheriff Caldwell spoke up in a gravelly voice. "Alex. Hi. How much data can we store with the, uh, database?"

"Depends on your server size, really. Although there are ways around that..."

"I guess what I'm driving at is we have lots of inmates who have short stays. And some move around a lot." He elbowed Charles in the ribs and smiled. "One guy I know can't seem to sit still for more than five minutes. Edgy Eddie's the name. Guys call him Edgy for short. Petty thief."

Sheriff Caldwell then leaned towards Drew. "I call him a pain in the..."

"Oh, it can handle it. Lots of real-time updating if you want." Alex flipped to another slide which showed a uniformed officer staring at a list of inmates on a computer monitor. "Even for thieves."

Alex eyed Charles leaning back in his chair, his mind obviously working on something big. He found himself overanalyzing Charles' mannerisms, now wondering how big of a prison he was really thinking of.

Charles said, "Okay, think big. Say, several thousand. Can it handle it?"

"Easily."

A snide smile crossed Charles' face.

"I must say I'm impressed," the sheriff said. "I'll have to have our IT gurus look over the specs."

Alex stared on at Charles a moment and then glanced at the sheriff. "Just out of curiosity, what kinds of criminals do you handle there?"

"Oh, all kinds. Thieves, drunks, druggies, thugs. Had a murder suspect last week."

"You guys ever investigate much? Like how some thieves get a hold of people's account info?"

"You mean like identity theft?"

"Right."

"Sometimes. It's frustrating work. Half the time we have no clue how they get people's info."

Alex glared back at Charles, who scribbled something or another on a piece of paper. "Ever work with payroll Charles?"

Charles looked up. "Payroll?" He drummed a pen on the tabletop. "I might bankroll the payroll but I don't cut the checks." He pointed at Drew. "That's his job."

Alex watched as Drew rolled his eyes. Then: "Ever dig around through people's belongings?"

Charles leaned back and adjusted his suit coat. He glanced at the sheriff and shook his head. "Me? No way, man."

Drew spoke up. "Is something the matter, Alex? Maybe we should talk outside the room later."

"Sounds like a plan."

* * *

Later in the afternoon, Alex stopped in the doorway of Drew's office. The man's office was a study in oak, books, boats, and fish. Behind his head and high upon the wall, was a mounted Northern pike

20

which was rumored to be nearly three feet long from mouth to tail, pulled from Vermilion Lake in northern Minnesota.

Below that and on both sides of him were two five foot high bookcases loaded down with business books, electronics books, and even a book on boat restoration. An entire shelf was devoted to nothing but biographies of business greats and celebrities. Pictures of his family adorned his desk, including a picture of his son behind the wheel of a replica 1800's schooner.

"Say, Drew," Alex said. "I was wondering how difficult it would be to change my direct deposit account number."

His boss appeared to be preoccupied with some paperwork on the desk. "Oh, it's quite easy. Just ask Becky for a direct deposit form." He then looked up. "Is this related to what you said earlier?"

Alex hedged a moment, looking off at a nearby cubicle wall, then back at his boss. "Somebody wrote some bad checks against my account and I had to close it down."

"Sorry to hear that. Did you call your bank?"

"Right away."

Drew took off his glasses and leaned back in his chair. He put his feet, tennis shoes and all, up onto his desk. "Were you thinking somebody here took your info?"

"It crossed my mind."

"Seriously? I mean, I can look into it, but Becky's the only one who works directly with anything like that. I don't think she'd do something like that, but I'll talk to her."

Alex let his shoulders deflate.

Drew lowered his voice and motioned for Alex to come closer. He put his feet down and leaned forward.

"Or were you thinking Charles was digging through your office?"

Alex stepped closer to Drew's desk. "I don't know. I mean, I shut my door and all that when I leave every night."

Drew nodded and leaned back. He then crossed his arms. "I'll keep my eye out for it. You can trust me on that. Now then, I'd talk to you some more, but I have a conference call to take. After all, everything comes to him who hustles while he waits. Know who said that?"

"No."

"Edison." Suddenly, Drew's telephone rang. He motioned towards Alex. "Let me know what happens."

Alex sighed. In his mind he ran through everybody in the company who had access to his checking account information. Somehow he sensed it was not Drew who concocted the fake checks. How would he stay in business like that? Besides, this company was Drew's second attempt at running a business, with the first attempt being a video rental store that was done in by haphazard bookkeeper. He thanked Drew and left the office.

As he returned to his own office, he packed up his belongings and shut down his computer for the day. He scooped up a few pieces of stray paper from his desk and left his office, closing the door behind him. He walked on towards the front door and attempted to stuff the papers into his briefcase.

A moment later, he opened the front door of the building. A gust of wind almost blew him back in. Dust blew around the parking lot and some of it flew up into his eyes. While he blinked and wiped the sand out of his eye, another gust of wind knocked the papers out of his hand and into the parking lot. Like thrown confetti, each piece went off in its own direction. He scrambled to catch and track down every loose piece of paper he could and brought the dirtied, crumpled remains back into his car.

Chapter Five

Upon arriving home that evening from work, Alex stopped at the foot of the driveway and checked the mailbox. He found four envelopes from the bank. He then drove into the garage and sat in his car. One by one, he ripped open the envelopes and examined the copies of the forged checks that he ordered last week.

All four looked like payroll checks, and all had signatures unlike his own. In the upper left hand corner on each one was his current address. Beneath that was his driver's license number, which never appeared on his checks. Three checks were for area gas stations, and one was from a nearby supermarket. The attempt to forge his signature appeared so awful that he figured a simple request by a clerk to see a means of identification would have nailed the crook on the spot. All around, the checks appeared to be the half-baked effort of an amateur.

He slipped out of his car and entered the house through the garage service door. With heavy steps he lumbered up the stairs and turned to climb the next set of stairs that led to the living room. He passed through the living room and into the dining room, where he slapped the bank paperwork onto the table and flipped on the light.

A brisk survey of the affidavit of forgery form revealed a place for his name, address, a description of the items forged, amounts, dates and questions about the payees listed on the checks. It also had room to write a chronology of events. On page four of the form it required his signature to be notarized. *That should be a dead giveaway*, he thought, *signing my name in front of a notary public.*

In his mind he continued to line up suspects against an imaginary wall and profiled them one by one. Who had access? The CamdenBank employees did. So did his previous landlord because Alex put quite a bit of information on their rental application and paid their apartment rent by check. That was over a year ago, however.

He strolled into the kitchen and poured himself a steaming cup of coffee. Out of the corner of his eye he saw his latest jigsaw puzzle sitting undisturbed on a brown card table in the corner of the kitchen. He walked over to it and admired it, even though it was only an eighth completed. He only had the top and bottom borders finished, and in that moment, found a piece that started to fill in one of the side borders. He plugged the piece into position and meandered back to the dining room table.

Just as he set his coffee mug down, the doorbell rang. He bounded downstairs to the front door, which was halfway between the living room and the stairs down to the garage. While peering through the security eyelet, he noticed it was a woman, with wavy, reddish-brown hair, and narrow oval eyeglasses. She was dressed in blue jeans and a black tee shirt, calmly staring off at the bushes in front of the house and then at the door again. Puzzled, he opened the door.

"Hi...I saw you lose these papers on your way to your car today." She extended a few crinkled sheets of paper out to Alex. "I was leaving a store nearby, but by the time I caught up to them, you had already left."

Alex snatched the papers out of her hand. They were printouts of electronic mail he received at work, one by accident, one on purpose. On one sheet was a prototypical sketch of the Pegasus ring, only next to it in the diagram was a smaller, disc-shaped chip sketched on the back of a human hand.

"Thanks," Alex said, and shut the door. In the stack of papers, he found a copy of a new direct deposit form he filled out for human resources earlier in the day. Unfortunately, another diagram was still missing.

He reopened the door, and the woman was still standing there, holding the other page. "Is that the rest of my stuff?"

"Yes, but..."

Alex put up a hand. "Sorry. It's just been a crazy week for me. A crazy couple of weeks for that matter."

"I can relate. Things are always frenzied for me."

"Frenzied?"

"Frantic. Chaotic. Wild."

"Ah."

Upon handing him the remaining sheets, Alex smirked and creased them. For the first time, he noticed the drawing on her tee shirt. It was a well-done, cartoon ink drawing of a man holding some type of pole and lighting an 1800's-era street lamp. Across the bottom of the shirt was the word "LAMPS" in all caps.

The woman put her hands in her pockets and rocked back and forth in her tennis shoes. "I don't mean to pry, but did you do that drawing?"

"Someone at work did. Frankly, I could not come up with something like that."

"Why's that?"

"It takes the phrase 'function creep' to a whole new level."

"But if it's so creepy, why do you work with it?"

"It's a long story. Interesting shirt by the way. Is that something custom?"

"It is. I do freehand sketching on the computer all the time."

"Can I ask what LAMPS stands for?"

"Sure you can ask."

There was a moment of silence. Alex smiled uncomfortably. "Okay. Let's try again. What does LAMPS stand for?"

"Leaders Against Mass Public Surveillance."

"Ah."

Alex began to turn away to close the door, but stopped a moment to think. "Say, don't you work down the road at the bookstore? Erin's Books, maybe?"

"I do...I remember you. Sorry, my name is Kay." She put forth a hand to shake, which Alex did.

"Nice to meet you, Kay. I'd stay and talk, but I'm in the middle of filling out some paperwork. Thanks again."

At once he closed the door.

Before the door was completely shut, however, he heard her say, "you're welcome, Alex."

He returned upstairs to the kitchen. He set his recovered paperwork into a new pile on the dining room table.

Danielle soon came up the stairs with a blue basket full of folded clothes in her arms. "Who was that?"

"Somebody from near my work. I, uh, dropped some papers in the parking lot."

Danielle nodded and reached the top of the stairs.

Alex suddenly bolted by her and lunged for the front door, swinging it open. He stepped out onto the front steps and then onto the sidewalk leading up to the house. In every direction the sidewalks were empty. "That was weird. I never told her my name."

"Secret admirer?"

"Wow. No. Hey, did you hear who's running our bank now?"

"Our bank?"

"I switched banks last week. James Malloy's president now."

"Your ex-boss?"

"Yeah. I talked to him. For a minute."

"I would have paid good money to see that."

"Right. A division by zero bug in my code single-handedly brought down a critical accounting app for almost a whole day. Jim never let me live that one down."

"Oh, that's right. And then, some wise guy went and printed up a bright red tee-shirt that said "Saved by Zero" in big white letters. Whatever happened to that shirt?"

"It disappeared mysteriously."

"Speaking of Jim, didn't you guys used to have a nickname for him?"

"Oh yes. They used to call him Slyhand."

Danielle nodded but looked confused as she lugged the laundry basket towards their bedroom.

"Know why they called him Slyhand?" Alex continued. "Quick with a guitar pick and even quicker to pick a pocket."

"Hopefully he's a changed man," she said, her voice full of sarcasm.

"Why change now? Now he's got millions to play with."

Alex then returned to the dining room table via the living room. On his way, he passed in between the couch and the bookcase. For a moment, he glanced over at some of his programming books and admired their titles. He also spotted the Bible, and for the first time in a long time, he felt a prompting to open it.

He then pushed that thought under and marched towards the table instead.

Chapter Six

Inside his spacious office, James Malloy peered over a paper version of the annual report for local rival CamdenBank. The cover art was pure marketing schmaltz, with a picture of several hands reaching up to touch one another and a cheesy tagline that read "We Can at Camden". His eyes glazed over with boredom just at the sheer size of the report. He flipped straight to the back of the report and scanned the numbers.

In the five-year summary section, he found several key figures sliding downhill. Deposits were dropping. Credit and debt card revenue was at a five-year low. Loan volume was also just beginning to drop, which brought a wide grin to his face. He wondered how much damage would show up on next year's report. Who knew corporate death could be so beautifully illustrated with graphs and pie charts?

He leaned back in his black leather chair and stared over to his left at the view through his bank of office windows. The Bloomington skyline was unexciting as usual. He reached over and grabbed a bright red cinnamon bear from the square, glass candy jar on the corner of his desk.

A moment later, he heard the click of the security lock on the heavy oak double doors off to the right of his desk and watched as Charles Lantham burst into the room without even a knock. Malloy stood up at his desk, hands in his pockets, and smiled. Charles was dressed in a dark blue dress shirt, tan khakis and a crimson tie.

"Sorry, I'm late. Traffic's nuts out there," he said, walking in with a swagger of someone twice his size. He seated himself in the middle of the three semicircular black leather chairs that were placed in an arc opposite of Malloy's desk. He set a black briefcase at his feet and opened it up to withdraw several papers. "Here's the latest specs for the Pegasus system."

Malloy reached over and took the papers, and examined them one by one. The papers were bound together by a black metal clip, which he unfastened. The top sheet showed an explosion diagram of the Pegasus ring. Next to that were the words "several thousand" written in pen and circled.

"This is more fun than annual reports," Malloy said. "Have you pitched my idea yet to your engineers?"

"I've dropped some hints. Don't worry. They're pushovers."

Malloy smirked and pointed his finger at Charles. "That's what I like to hear."

He sat back down in his chair and put his feet up on his desk. He stared straight ahead at Charles with an intensity that could easily ignite the bookcases behind the man's chair. "I can't believe how well things have gone so far. Have you checked the papers? CamdenBank stock is down twenty-five percent in one week. *One week!* A manager told me West Pines Credit Union has lost *two hundred* customers this month alone. Two hundred, my friend."

"But are you selling your cards?"

"Am I selling cards." Malloy shook his head and laughed. "The uptake on Liberty Cards has been fabulous. But you know a retail version of your tech will be our ace in the hole."

Charles flashed a sarcastic smile.

"What was that for?" Malloy said, studying Charles' features.

Charles sighed. "On the phone last week you said you wanted the system to track tens of thousands. This morning, you upped it to millions."

"Millions is right. If your engineers aren't up to it, I'll find someone else."

"No, no. We got it."

"If you don't tell me now. I have another company at work on something even bigger. I don't think the customers are ready for it though."

"What's that?"

"Implanted chips."

At that Malloy heard the click of the security lock on his double doors again. In walked his administrative assistant, Susan, with an unlabeled manila folder in her hand. Malloy smiled at her, as she set it on the corner of his desk and headed back towards the door.

"Lunch today, Susan?" He said, interlacing his hands to form a steeple.

"I'm leaving at noon, Jim."

She had shoulder length platinum blonde hair and bottomless blue eyes one could practically drown in. Malloy eyed her figure and her red, blue, and yellow print dress all the way out the door. He noticed Charles watching her, too, and when she left, he glanced for a moment inside the manila folder.

"That woman breaks my heart. Always playing hard to get. Makes for a good chase, though."

Charles drew back and grimaced. "She smells like vanilla."

"Some kind of perfume I think. I think it's great." Malloy leaned over and opened his candy jar. "Cinnamon bear?"

Charles waved him off.

Malloy then stood up from his chair and paced over to a window. He spread out his arms as if gesturing to an audience outside. "Can you just imagine it one day? I could sit up here in my office without ever leaving my chair and learn more about the people in this town than the cops could gather in a lifetime of work."

"How so?"

"Soon I'll be able to track almost anyone. Where they shop, where they eat, what they do for fun." Malloy turned his back to the window and pointed at Charles. "In fact, show me a person's checkbook and I'll show you where their loyalty lies. And once you know their loyalty, they all become pushovers."

"Really? So what's my loyalty? What's *my* motivation?"

Malloy stuffed a cinnamon bear into his mouth. "Money."

Charles sat silent a moment and then said with a sly grin, "I guess you're right."

* * *

Later that evening, Malloy pulled off the highway and onto Main Street to head towards Anoka. He drove along Main Street for a few miles, passing by numerous strip malls, department stores, restaurants, and banks. As he waited at different stoplights, for the fun of it he tried to figure each business' net worth, as if he were bidding on parts of a giant Monopoly board.

All that changed when he entered Anoka itself and found a mix of homes, townhomes, restaurants, and small businesses next to one another. He took a left at the Fourth Avenue stoplight and rolled down a quiet residential street. On his left was a pill-shaped athletic field with a large set of bleachers on one side. Just beyond that, the city's water tower loomed like a giant, silver jellyfish under the bright August moon.

He slowed his car to a crawl as he passed by the parking lot of the Anoka Middle School for the Arts. He checked the time on his car clock and squinted to see if his contact would be hanging around the building as previously agreed. He was in luck as he spied a lone figure doing skateboard stunts near the front doors of the school.

He wheeled into the parking lot, but he knew his time here would have to be short as not to draw suspicion from the local police department. He parked and got out of his car, surveying his surroundings every step of the way. He approached the young man who continued to ride his skateboard along the sidewalk. The young man stood a skinny six-foot-two, with a surfer-blonde style haircut, and wore a ragged plaid shirt and torn jeans.

"Evening, Ben," Malloy said, standing near a square trash container.

Ben kept skateboarding.

"I'll keep this short. Here's the deal as I envision it. You and I both know your Dad got a bum rap when he was sent off. Now I know some people over in the Walworth system who could make sure your dad gets a get out of jail free card if you know what I mean."

Ben stopped a moment to listen, and held onto his board.

"It breaks my heart to see a fine citizen like that shafted by the system. But to get from here to there I need you to do me a little favor. I have a bit of a cleanup operation in mind. But in order to pull it off, I'm going to need it to be done in a way that's untraceable. That's where you come in. You're good with chemistry right?"

Ben snapped his skateboard back onto the pavement and pushed off.

Malloy looked back towards his car and scanned the street. "Okay. Here's the deal. I need you to take down one of my branches. The old one over in Plymouth. We inherited it from a merger. The place is a dump anyway."

Malloy stood there a moment, awaiting a response. Down the street, he heard a car pass by and he glanced to see what kind of vehicle it was. The only other sound was the steady clink-clink of the wind blowing the flagpole cord against the pole nearby.

At this point, he shrugged his shoulders and paced towards his car. He turned to point a finger back at Ben. "You think about what I said."

Ben kept skateboarding.

Upon reaching the car and opening the door, Malloy heard a voice shouting from behind him.

"What makes y'all think I care?"

Malloy spun back around. "Ever talk much to your friend Sean Oliver? Well you and I both know he's got a bit of a...what do you call it? A record? Maybe you should see what he's been up to lately. Ask him what happened when he tried to screw over one of my branch managers. He was a real piece of work. He learned fast. You could learn something from him."

At that Malloy got into his car and slammed his door shut. He admired himself in his rear view mirror. "Thank you. Thank you very much," he said to himself in his best Elvis voice, as he slipped an Elvis CD into his stereo. He then sped off as the first bars of Viva Las Vegas rang out from his speakers.

Chapter Seven

The following morning Alex stopped in at Abernathy's supermarket a mile or so down the road from his house. He entered through the outer automatic sliding doors of the store, passed lines of shopping carts to his right, and entered through another set of sliding doors. At first, he stood a bit bewildered because he did not normally shop here.

To his right was the produce section, with a bright, colorful assortment of apples, oranges, and many types of vegetables. To his left, he noticed a row of checkout lanes, two-thirds of which were staffed by cashiers wearing pale red shirts and black pants. He began to walk towards one of the cashiers, but then eyed a small floral section on the left side of the store across from the checkout lanes. Next, he came upon a set of restrooms, an in-store bank, and finally the employee break room.

He noticed a man wearing a red employee shirt and reading a newspaper at one of the tables. He poked his head into the doorway and altered his normally deep, but nasally, voice. "Break time's up, buddy. Let's go."

At that he ducked back out into the store and pretended to look busy staring at a nearby soda vending machine. He reached into his pocket for some change. A moment later the employee burst out of the break room but came to a stop by the vending machine.

"The machine works better if you put money in the dollar bill slot," the employee said, standing next to Alex. "Although rumor has it if you hit the first and second buttons at the same time, it just might give you a free pop."

"But everything's sold out. And I'm not drinking bottled water. Personally, I'd like to file a protest with the management. Or I'll make a scene."

"You're talking to the right man. Follow me upstairs, sir."

At that, Alex followed his old college friend, Ian, who worked as a tech troubleshooter for the store chain. Ian stood a lean six-foot-three, with short, brown hair and a leisurely gait. He seemed to have a continual Bill Murray-like smirk on his face and was always hitting his head on something or another. Together, they hiked up a set of stairs to the management offices, which sat empty this morning. Ian opened the office door and Alex followed him inside.

Alex glanced around to see several towering file cabinets, an old time card rack, and an obsolete punch clock. On the desk in front of him were a pair of computer screens with eight different camera views of the store that switched every thirty seconds. The cameras themselves were encased in black globes that hung from the ceiling throughout the store, prowling over shoppers like an array of beach-ball-sized bug eyes.

Alex withdrew a photocopy of one of the forged checks and stared again at the slightly smudged endorsement stamp on the back of the check. He then looked over the payee line on the front and handed the paper over to Ian. "So, could you find this guy? The one that wrote this check?"

Ian grabbed the paper from Alex. "Probably, if you give me a day or two. I'll line up the dollar amount with the purchases that day and then see if I can match it up with the security video."

Alex looked around the office a bit. To the left of the desk where the security computer sat was another PC tower with its case removed. Next to that was a black, cloth bag full of tools, and to the left of that was a box of opened chocolate doughnuts. Alex helped himself to one as Ian continued to study the check copy.

"I just read in the paper that another bank was hit yesterday," Ian said after a moment.

"Any clues?"

"No, Although another stolen laptop was involved."

"It's funny you mention that. I saw one the other day just sitting at a table in a gas station. No one was near it."

"What color was it?"

"Black, I think. Like the one I have at home."

Ian looked up at Alex.

"What?"

"I read a post online last night suggesting some of the laptops may have been planted. I'll double check on that before I start that rumor circulating."

Alex began to examine the PC tower without the cover.

"Hey, you want to see the pride of Abernathy's management? C'mere. It's our purchase tracking system. All items that pass over our scanners at the registers are recorded here," Ian said.

Ian switched one of the computer monitor views over to some sort of system screen and pointed at it. "See, it helps in the tracking of sales volume, inventory and creating coupons at the register. Supposedly, it's purged of customer information more than three years old, but it's been up for five years running. In fact, the sack of Alpo dog food I bought five years ago is still in the database. Can't think of anything I've bought in this store since then."

Ian tapped away at the black keys of the keyboard. "Talk about putting information together. Go over to the window. See Mrs. Hill over there at register two? She's down there wearing a white tee-shirt and blue shorts."

Alex stood up and edged himself between the computer desk and a filing cabinet, staring out into the vastness of the supermarket.

"Here's her shopping list item by item in real time. There goes a bag of cat food over the scanner. And a gallon of two percent milk."

"How did ya know who it was?"

"Two ways. We have a shopper savings card system, and of course, I can look over here at the camera. When they swipe that shoppers card through, her name pops up over here. Besides, I've seen her in here a million times."

"So you basically know everything she put in her cart just by sitting up here?"

"Sure. If I am really bored I suppose I could try to pull up what she has purchased over the past year."

Alex continued to stare down at the maze of aisles and registers, and watched a pony-tailed brunette in a tan coat weave her way from freezer case to freezer case.

"There goes a loaf of bread. And a bottle of vitamins. And look at that…denture cleaner. I wonder when she got those?"

Alex spun around to see Ian smiling.

"Hey, did I ever tell you about our KartBuddy system?" Ian asked.

"No."

"It was a system where we tagged goods in the store with RFID tags. When you put the items in the cart, it'd ring it up and calculate all sorts of figures for you. Total price, blah, blah, blah. Who knows. Maybe it would even balance your checkbook for you if you gave it a chance."

"Sounds creative."

"Here's the best part. Each buddy had a big range and could show you where the products were in the store. It'd tell you the aisle number and all that."

Ian paused and kicked back in his chair.

"Then what happened?" Alex said.

"We had an electrical storm one night. A few KartBuddies were left out in the rain and went batty. They started reporting all sorts of aisle numbers like 510, 650, and 817. It even reported a can of peas in aisle 2,367."

"You know, some days I can't tell when you make stuff up."

"True story. Honest. No more KartBuddies."

Alex went back by Ian and looked down at his feet to see Ian's black work bag on the floor. He caught a glimpse of a yellow-colored CD case, with the wording "Atari 80 Classic Games in One" on the side. He reached down and withdrew the CD. "Just like old times, eh?"

"Remember those days? But you know what I remember? When it came to cracking and swapping games, you had no equal."

"You still do that?"

Ian smirked. "Maybe. Maybe not. You?"

"No. I stopped that a long time ago."

"When did that happen?"

Alex set the CD back into Ian's bag. He turned back to look through the one-way windows and out onto the store floor. The view was impressive from up here.

"Wait, don't tell me. You had a Jesus moment."

"Ian, I've had those for a while. I just never talked about it much. God even bugged me the other day to read the Bible again. I'll get to it someday if I can."

"Well, if you ever want to hang out at some forums with me or go to a gaming convention, just look me up."

Alex smiled in return.

"Okay, well, I'll see what I can do about this," Ian said after a moment.

"Thanks, man. I owe you one."

"I hope you know I'm kidding about the Jesus moment thing. Oh, and on your drive out of the parking lot be sure to check out Abernathy's own radio station."

Alex grabbed the door handle and began to leave the office. "Abernathy's radio station?"

"Sure. It's low-range. Only goes out about a half mile at most. It's at 107.5 FM. It's got like Muzak or something and then they talk about our specials. Oh, and recipes, too."

Alex grinned as if to say, "yeah, right."

"True story. Honest," Ian said.

"How long do you expect that to last?"

"I give it a month. Tops."

* * *

Soon Alex arrived back home and tossed his car keys on the coffee table in the living room. The living room had a bright, open feel to it because all the windows were open as well as the curtains. Danielle reclined on the couch, flipping through a seed catalog. The coffee table was covered in seed packets, used starter pots, and a couple of gardening books from the library.

"Any luck?" She asked him.

"Lots of it. Ian thinks he can find the guy."

"Then what?"

"Good question."

"It's not like you could confront the guy on the street. What if he's a drug addict? What if he's twice your size and his arms are covered in tattoos and he rides a motorbike?"

"I'd still confront him." He meandered into the kitchen and stared on at his jigsaw puzzle. He pulled a chair out of the dining room and sat down in front of the card table. With ease, he began sorting out the edge pieces into a neat pile. With navy blue, dark blue, and white sea foam pieces he began to assemble the outer edges of an ocean scene.

"That store is weird," he said after a moment of thought.

"Which one?"

"Abernathy's. I've never looked out on the store from above like that. It was like I watching over a big lab experiment."

Chapter Eight

Over a week went by before Alex heard from Ian again. In his plastic desktop inbox that morning he found a five-page facsimile from his friend. On one page was a fuzzy image of a man at the checkout register. The angle was poor and he could only make out a rough guess as to what the figure looked like in person. It looked like a teenager or maybe a man in his early twenties, with almost no hair and vacant eyes. He let his tense shoulders uncoil a moment as it did not look like anybody he knew.

He stood up from his desk and glanced around his office. In front of him, on his L-shaped desk, two computers compiled away on separate projects—one was a Mac, and the other a PC. Behind him were two bookcases, two-thirds full of programming books, and on top of one of them was a stuffed Tux penguin. On his wall were two Visual Studio posters and a pair of framed pictures of Caribbean beaches.

He left his office and walked out into the central part of his company's office, where there were eight cubicles clustered together along with a copier, a fax machine, a laser printer, and a reception desk near the front door.

In front of the laser printer, he waited quietly for his job to print. Page after page poured out, none of which were his. Then the printer paused and whirred again. One page came out by itself. From the back it looked like a memo. Warm to the touch, he turned it over and skimmed its contents.

From: Charles Lantham, Sales
To: Drew Arthur

Drew,

Here is another idea for the Pegasus ring…could we change the color of it? To say, brighter colors? I have an idea that would give us a foothold in the retail sector. We could turn the rings into bracelets, sort of like a wrist-credit card. What do you think?

Charles

Alex dropped the memo back onto the printer tray and grabbed his screen print which dropped down on top. He waited a moment to see if Charles would come out of his office, but his colleague's door remained closed. Upon returning to his own office, he scribbled down all he could remember. He did not know at the moment whether to like or hate the idea of a "wrist credit card", much less come up with a way to implement a solution, if asked. He looked again at Ian's fax.

"Lydia," he called out.

Lydia, the company's administrative assistant, relationship advisor and collector of arcane cookbooks slipped into his doorway moments later. "Missing a page?"

"No. You remember when that roofing contractor stole your checks a few years ago?"

She came into his office and stood in front of his desk, with her hands on her hips. "Like yesterday. Is your roof leaking?" She had a heavy Caribbean accent, a new perm, and wore a bright green and black plaid sundress. For a moment, she toyed with one of her silver hoop earrings.

"No, but somebody hit my account about a couple weeks ago."

"No. Get out of town."

"How did the contractor get your info?"

"The detective told me he probably got it by digging through my trash. Tell me what happened."

"I don't know. I filled my car up over at the Pit Stop and the next thing I knew my card was no good."

Lydia stared on at Alex, and then sat on the edge of his desk. "Did you call the bank? 'Cause that's what I did. I called 'em up and gave them an earful. You shoulda heard me."

"Yeah, I called the bank."

Alex noticed her leaning towards him, nearly knocking over a picture of his wife. He leaned back in his chair. "Um, do you mind not sitting on my desk?"

"Sure thing, honey."

A moment later, Charles burst into the doorway of Alex's office, drumming his fingers against the door frame. He eyed Lydia's figure and smiled. "Hey bud, could ya run a report for me? I sent you a list of requirements. Check your e-mail. Thanks, buddy."

Alex peered back down at his monitor and opened the note from Charles.

Lydia turned to leave his office. "Buddy? Since when did you two become best friends?"

"Since he wanted something from me."

* * *

An hour later Alex lounged in Drew's office, with Charles nearby, listening. Compared to Alex's office, Drew's office felt more outdoors-like, with his mounted fish on the wall and numerous fake plants on the floor. Charles sat in a chair next to Alex, wearing a white dress shirt, black dress pants, and a Minnesota Wild hockey tie.

"Alex," Charles said, leaning forward in his chair, "We're looking to expand the Pegasus technology in new directions. We've had a handful of other companies showing great interest. Some retail interest, too."

"Pegasus is built for prisons, not retail. When you start heading into the retail sector, then you have to worry a lot more about encryption, access rights, bigger networks..."

"Lemme elaborate. One deal we're working on involves Jenson's grocery chain. They want to do something as a pilot program. Now I was talking to Steven Wick, and he oversees the marketing over there at Jenson's corporate office..."

Alex zoned out a moment and immediately thought of Ian. The ease that his friend moved through the screens and moved through the data, combined with a concept like the Pegasus chip, made him squirm in his chair now. Distracted, he stared off at a fake plant in the corner.

"Something wrong?" Charles said.

"No, keep going."

"Then there's our big catch. Aspirizon Bank."

Alex sat up straight. "Wait. What would they need that for?"

"Their president has got some great ideas for the future." Charles emphasized the word 'great' with an affirmative head nod, as if that helped.

Alex rubbed his eyes. "Let's get the basic tech right before we go that far. You're talking about a complete rethinking of purpose. Hardly an overnight process."

Drew leaned forward in his chair, as if he suddenly came to life. "Of course not and nobody is expecting that. You realize, though, if we do not take advantage of this opportunity, somebody else will. Charles has convinced me of that. There's a great deal of interest in what we've done. Charles is putting together quite an impressive list of potential clients to market to. Besides, it would be nice to stir up a little talk in trade press."

Alex brooded.

"Of course, none of this is final," Charles jumped in. He leaned back in his chair and interlaced his hands as if to pray. "So what do I tell my sales staff? That it's impossible? That you're not up to the task?"

"Start with hardware, Chuck," Alex said.

Suddenly, Charles' hands sprung apart like a jack-in-the-box. "You're unbelievable. Just unbelievable. This is our big chance to score and instead of taking a shot you cave."

"I'm not caving. And this isn't hockey."

"Alex, we're going forward on this," Drew said, turning to look at something on his computer monitor.

In the background, Alex heard his desk phone ringing. He seized the moment and turned it into a chance to escape. "Sorry guys, but I have some phone messages and e-mail to catch up on. If you gentleman will excuse me, I'll attend to that." Without another word he strode out of the office and fled to the tentative security of his own office.

As he shut his office door, he took a deep breath and sighed. *Now what was old Slyhand up to?*

He settled back into his chair and picked up the phone.

"Alex? It's Danielle. Do you know where we put David's backpack?"

"Good question. I think it's in his closet."

"Got it. Thanks."

"Tell him to have a great first day of Kindergarten."

"I will. Love ya."

"Love ya, too."

At that, Alex hung up the phone and withdrew a piece of paper from inside his desk. Lydia's last day as a Hoyle-Aspen employee was fast approaching, and he made a note to himself to pick her up a gift for her departure on behalf of the entire staff. He then glanced over at some new images Ian just faxed over to him.

In these shots, it became clear the person who hit his account was a teenager. Alex wondered if this kid found an abandoned laptop like Ian suggested. *He sure doesn't look like somebody who is savvy with a computer*, thought Alex. *After all, the kid passed a bunch of bum checks.*

Staring hard at one of the pages, he intended to memorize the face and memorize it well.

Chapter Nine

Ben sat alone in his basement bedroom, with his stereo turned up. The lone window in the room was taped over with a black trash bag to "keep out the light while he slept". Or so he told his mother. The rest of his room was painted a dark blue, with black carpeting. His walls were plastered over with various rock band posters, a Tony Hawk poster, and in one corner, a table of elements diagram.

He sat at his desk now and ignored his college homework and instead focused on a map of Aspirizon branch #273 in Plymouth. There was one main entrance to the bank, a lobby, an area of banker's desks, and of course, the teller area. He could not tell from the map if they had a drive-thru or not. With his finger he traced out paths through the building. Likely the building would have a brick exterior, so it would be a difficult job at best.

He reached into his top desk drawer and pulled out a small, clear, plastic tube filled with kerosene and a tiny piece of sodium. In its purest form, sodium could be quite reactive with the surrounding air, causing it to explode violently and even ignite under the right conditions. He rolled the tube between his fingertips and daydreamed if there was a way he could work this idea into the job.

Over the sound of his stereo, he heard the telephone ring. He dropped the tube back into his desk, along with the map, and slammed the drawer shut. On the third ring he picked up the phone near his bed and powered down his stereo.

"Hello?"

"Hey, Ben it's Sean. You droppin' by tonight?"

"Maybe later. I gots somethin' to do first."

"Like what?"

Ben could hear the laughter of a girl in the background. "A favor for someone. I'll call you in a bit."

At that, he hung up the phone. Already, his palms began to sweat.

His heart jack-hammered away in his chest. Normally this feeling did not hit him until it was time to pull off a job. He ran a hand through his hair and changed into a pair of faded jeans and a blue and black polo shirt. He glanced over at his desk and especially at the stack of chemistry books, and then his skateboard leaning against the wall.

Next to the desk, of course, were several model rockets, and next to those in a closed cardboard box were numerous rocket engines and chutes. On his bookshelf next to that were several three-ring binders full of diagrams, ideas and designs for new types of engines.

He returned to his desk and locked it up. After a minute of pacing back and forth, he left his room. Three times he reopened his bedroom door and checked the lock on his desk and the locks on the drawers under his waterbed. Three more times he locked his bedroom door. Only then did he head upstairs. On the way out the door, he found a note on the kitchen table from his mother. She would be coming home late from work. This was a good thing he reasoned, because the fewer explanations he had to make today, the better.

* * *

Ben pulled into the parking lot of the bank branch and climbed out of his black, rusted Toyota Camry. In seconds, he surveyed the landscape around the bank. He carried a Folgers coffee can full of change under his arm, which would buy him some time with the teller. In his pocket, he stuffed several twenty dollar bills and a birthday check he had yet to cash.

He entered the lobby of the bank and was immediately struck by the odor of fresh popcorn. It nearly made him gag. Surveying the interior, he found it matched up perfectly with the map he looked over an hour earlier. It was a converted branch, and high up on one of the walls he could see the faint outlines of the old bank's name: Westwind Bank. Off to his left were the banker's desks and a fake floor plant next to each one of them. The plant pots looked to be filled with some type of stringy material. In other words, it was a perfect place for dropping an errant cigarette.

Perfect for kindling.

He walked over to the teller line and noticed a man in his eighties, repeatedly asking the lone Asian female teller about the balance on

44

his account. In the meantime, his eyes swept over the floor, then along the walls and across the ceiling. There were cameras everywhere.

Once the man in front of him finished his business, he approached the Asian woman. She appeared to be in her mid-twenties, and was quite beautiful, although her shoulder length haircut bothered him. He set his can of coins on her counter and dug into his pants pockets for the bills and the birthday check. The sound of his own heartbeat flooded his ears.

"Good afternoon," the teller said.

"Hi. I have some change I'd like to cash and bills to convert."

"Do you have an account with us?"

She was sweet. Really. Hopefully she would not be working late in a few weeks.

"No, I don't. Do I need one?" Ben replied.

"No, no. Here, I'll take that."

Her lipstick was right, though. He gave her that much. As she turned her back towards him carrying the coffee can, he scanned behind the counter for piles of paper or electrical devices that could potentially fail. He caught a glimpse of an aging coffee maker off to his right on a small wooden table. The cord running from the coffee maker to the wall even looked like it had been taped over in a couple of places with black electrical tape. It was a perfect candidate for after hours ignition. The paper filters, napkins, and paper cups next to it?

Perfect for kindling.

The coin counting machine finished in under a minute. The teller came back with a receipt and a smile that distracted him. She set his can on the counter and giggled. "It doesn't like washers and Canadian."

"Aw, that's just my dumb luck."

The teller giggled again. "Can I ask where you're from? I like your accent."

"I like yours, too, ma'am. I'm from Missoura."

"Missoura? Oh, you must mean Missouri."

Ben grabbed the can and jostled four washers inside and a couple of dimes. He then set his birthday check on the counter, along with a driver's license and a short stack of twenty dollar bills.

"More?"

"Yep," Ben said with a smile. "I'd like to convert these here into

Benjamins."

"Benjamins?"

"Hundreds."

The teller giggled again and blushed. "I knew what you meant."

As she picked up the stack of twenty dollar bills, she rearranged and rotated each bill into their proper alignment. Ben eyed the lobby some more. He was sure there was thorough camera coverage around the walls of the building, too. The windows looked quite durable, so a Molotov cocktail might be out of the question. He noticed some bushes through one window near a banker, however.

In seconds, the teller finished her counting, cashed his check, and counted the hundred dollar bills out on the counter before him. "Was there anything else?"

"Naw, I'm good. Thanks."

"Don't spend it all in one place," she said with a laugh. He joined in on the laughter, even though he did not feel like it. That haircut, though, had to change.

As he paced towards the exit, he ran into a woman in her thirties, with wavy brown hair and a five-year-old boy in tow. "Excuse me, ma'am," he said, still looking down and stuffing money into his wallet.

"Sorry," the woman said.

She was polite, beautiful and preoccupied herself with her son and her purse. The boy stared at him, however, and that was not good. He had seen that type of stare before.

As the woman and her son approached the open teller window, he heard the teller call out, "Good afternoon, Mrs. Poole. How are you?"

"Great, thanks," Mrs. Poole replied.

Ben continued on to the lobby door but heard the boy whisper something to his mother. He strained to listen, but only heard her reply, "We don't tell people they have creepy eyes. That's not polite."

He chuckled to himself.

At that he exited the bank and eyed the trees around the bank and then the wood chips all around the front portion of the building. He noticed a tiny pond in between two of the trees. He gauged its distance from the street. It was the perfect place to test his sodium-water device he was developing in his bedroom. And, if he approached it right, he could throw a perfect strike at the pond from

46

his car window. Doubtless something on the nearby roof would catch fire as well. The wood chips, the pond, the trees—the setup was perfect.

Perfect for kindling.

Chapter Ten

The following Friday afternoon Alex stopped in at Erin's Books. Located on the corner of a suburban strip mall in Woodbury, from the outside the store seemed dwarfed by the larger department stores next to it. Once he went inside, however, the store had an open feel, with numerous bookshelves in a pattern that probably resembled a piece of parquet flooring.

To his right, and near the entrance, he spotted a display that contained all sorts of well-drawn comic book art in a glass display case. Some of it appeared to have been created and signed by Kay herself. Up high and around the perimeter of the store, he also noticed yellow, marigold, and red paper leaves dotting the walls. In the corners of the store were red, shell-shaped cloth chairs that looked like they just flew off of a Tilt-A-Whirl ride. The chairs sat around small, round, wooden tables and the aroma of fresh-brewed coffee hung in the air.

He took in the category names above each section of books and eyed the sales counter in the middle of the store. There, Kay sat on a wooden barstool, reading *Wuthering Heights*. Her hair was done up in a braid this time, but she still had the same oval glasses, and was wearing a mulberry colored sweater.

Just as she started to look up from her book, he darted into an aisle. He wove between the bookshelves, scanning the titles and category tags on each shelf. He pulled out a hardcover picture book on the American Civil War and flipped through its pages. Disinterested, he slid it back into place. In another aisle, he browsed the titles devoted to the latest office software. Then he began to wonder who he was really buying a book for—Lydia or himself. Turning around, he stared at Kay and called out to her.

"I forgot to ask you the other day. How did you know my name?"

She did not look up from her book. "It was on one of the sheets you dropped."

"Do you always read people's personal materials?"

"No, but I do try to return them."

"Just checking."

Alex withdrew a tome on soup. Nothing but soups and more soups. Soups with exotic ingredients. Soups made with spices you would use once and then shelve until someone bought you a new spice rack. *Pictures of soup better left imagined than actually photographed,* Alex thought. *Cold soup, hot soup, cream soup, chunky soup.* Lydia loved soup, but not that much.

Kay suddenly looked up from her book. "Can I ask again what those pictures were about? It's been on my heart ever since to ask."

"Work projects. I didn't draw the hand thing, though."

"Okay, but when you saw it, were you curious in a technical sense or did you find it disconcerting?"

"Disconcerting?"

"Did it bug you?"

"What? The diagrams? Maybe a little."

Kay set down her novel, sliding a bookmark in place. "Alex, have you ever heard of the book of Revelation?"

"Sure."

He withdrew yet another book, then looked on at her a moment, confused. Then: "You mean the part about the mark in the hand or on the forehead?"

"Right."

"Oh, hey. That's not what was discussed. At least they didn't talk about it in front of me."

"Sorry, but that's the first thought that came into my mind when I saw that diagram."

"Well, like I said, certain salespeople get to sketching sometimes, and that kind of thing gets out of hand in a hurry. I can't imagine that kind of thing anyway. I'd think it'd be painful to implant. Besides, I don't think my company is important enough to be part of something foretold two thousand years ago."

He tried to laugh it off. Her facial expression remained unchanged, though.

"All it takes is an idea," she said.

An uneasy smile came over his face. "True. Oh, but we do other things, too."

What was the use? He had the same feeling wash over him when he first saw the ring memo. He cradled another book in his hands, and walked up to the register. Without thinking, he set it on the counter.

"Easy Crocheting?" She said.

Alex glared down at the book. "Ack. I thought I grabbed a cookbook. Honest. I got distracted."

"It's okay," she grinned. "I can put it back. Go look again. I'm not going anywhere."

"I'll put it back."

Alex returned it to the bookshelf and turned towards the cookbook section again. He discovered other cookbooks beneath the ones he looked at previously. He remembered now that Lydia was born on the island of St. Thomas and moved to the States a few years ago with her son, but harbored only cursory knowledge of American cooking. He paged through several volumes and decided on a general cookbook and approached the register again.

Kay rang up the purchase, bagged it, and handed a credit slip back to Alex to sign. When she handed him the bag, her hazel eyes seemed to pierce Alex right where it mattered most. She then held out a crème-colored pamphlet with brown lettering and added, "By the way, maybe this would explain my point better. Here, take one."

He reached for the pamphlet and turned it over in his hands. "What is it?"

"Read it. Take it home with you. You might learn something new."

He noticed a small logo on it with the word "LAMPS" beneath it. The logo was that of a person lighting a streetlamp again. On the counter next to the register, he saw a short stack of compact disc jewel cases. He noticed the same logo on there, too.

"Go on. Take one. It's an educational game," she said.

Alex grinned and read the back cover of the disc case. "Is it free?"

"For now. My brother writes games in his spare time. He's trying to establish himself in the industry."

"Maybe David would like it."

"David?"

"My son. Just started grade school."

"Brian's trying to get some early feedback on it, so let me know how it goes."

"Brian?"

"My brother."

"Ah. So it's a beta release."

"What?"

"A beta release. It's a term used for software that's not done. It's a bit unstable, but all of the features are there. You should really warn people about that on here. If it wrecks something, they'll come back to you."

"Well, he does not want me giving it out to anyone just yet."

"Yet you trust me with it? You don't even know me."

"The Lord said it was okay."

"Interesting."

Alex clutched the disc and headed to the door. As he leaned on the front door of the store, he stared at the back cover of the disc again. "Hold it. This is bugging me. Why do you have the same logo on here that you had on your shirt a ways back?"

"It's not what you think. But read the brochure."

Alex nodded, still unsure what to think, and stepped out into the parking lot.

Chapter Eleven

A week later Malloy met with Charles again in Malloy's office. Malloy carried in a box of pizza from the pizzeria across the street and popped open the box on his desk. He tore off a frigid Coke from a six pack on his desk and tossed a can to Charles, who sat in one of the semi-circular chairs in front of Malloy's desk. Again, Malloy took a handful of diagrams from Charles and peered over them with guarded interest.

"So what's the latest? Are your engineers on board?"

Charles snapped open his Coke, grabbed two slices of pepperoni, sausage, and mushroom pizza and slapped the pieces down on a paper plate. He then took a bite of pizza followed by a swig of soda. "I don't know. One of them is not too crazy about the retail rings. Drew's on board, though."

Malloy withdrew a pen from his desk drawer and began taking notes on a yellow legal pad. "What's the name of the engineer?"

"Poole. Alex Poole."

He wrote down Alex's name and then set his pen down. A wicked smile crossed his face. "Really? I didn't know he worked for you. Tell me more."

"Yeah. He's an engineer or whatever. He's a pretty smart guy."

"He ain't that smart." Malloy jotted more notes to himself on the legal pad. "Come to think of it, I saw him a while back. He stopped into the branch for something or another. Wanna know something? If you wanna watch him squirm, just ask him about the day he brought down the accounting department at the bank."

"That bad, huh?"

Malloy leaned back in his chair and reflected a moment. "I think I know why he's giving you a hard time."

"Why?"

"He's a Christian isn't he?"

Charles ate some more pizza then leaned forward. "I'm not sure. I think so."

"That's a pity. Funny. All the time I worked with him he rarely showed it. He never struck me as one. Later on I saw him coming out of a church."

Malloy stood up and admired a framed poster on the wall just behind him. It was a picture of the lead guitarist of a local hard rock band shuffling across a smoky lighted stage. At the bottom, in the lower right hand corner was the guitarist's signature. Malloy stuffed his hands into his suit pants pockets. He motioned towards the wall. "A poster like this would probably give him the heebie-jeebies. Ever seen these guys in concert?"

"No. I had tickets one time. Had to give them up."

Malloy strolled over to a guitar stand to the right of his desk and against the wall.

Charles laughed. "You leave that poster up there all the time?"

"Nah. Most of the time it stays up. Other times I have to take it down and replace it with a picture of Niagara Falls. Depends on the company that arrives." He picked up his Gibson six-string acoustic guitar from the stand and slipped the strap over his shoulder. He plucked the A string, and adjusted the tuning peg a half-twist. From there he walked back towards the window.

"Aren't you gonna have something to eat?" Charles said, lunging for a third piece of pizza.

"In a minute."

Malloy stood at the window and stared out onto the city. The skies clouded over now, and in the distance he could see rain streamers falling from a bank of dark blue and gray clouds. He strummed out the opening bars of *Stairway to Heaven* for the fun of it.

"I doubt Alex would like what I've got going on over at Lindemeier." Malloy said. "With the chips and all that."

"The chips?"

"Implanted chips. Well, we're testing wearable chips for now. Hey, maybe with some leverage ol' Alex would come around to the bracelets."

"All I know is, the guy drives me up the wall some days."

Malloy turned around to see Charles leaning back in his chair and stretching his legs out.

"Here's the thing. People like him give into peer pressure. Remember what I said about loyalty and being a pushover? He's a pushover of the highest order. But people like him have a flock mentality if you know what I mean. You gotta crack their ranks."

"That oughta be interesting."

"Listen, he may be come off like a bright guy, but deep down he can't think a whole lot for himself. Me, I think out of the box all the time. Guys like him need rules. Guys like him play it safe. And then they have the gall to tell you how to live your life. Or what music you should listen to."

Malloy strutted across the room and stood behind his desk. "But see, I'm already a step ahead of them. The key is not to give in to them. You hear me? Don't give in."

"The guy's got a lot of street cred with the boss."

"Oh, who cares. Here, try this angle. Say, *hey Drew...imagine this.* You walk into a mall, and stop in at the service desk. You walk around with no cash, no credit cards. Nothing but a bracelet. Like our Pegasus bracelet, but modified. Make it sleeker. More colorful. Then you shop around the mall, and it's a piece of cake. No signatures, no receipts."

Charles downed more pizza but remained silent.

"That's thinking out of the box. If your boss can't get on board with that, maybe he should find a new engineer."

Charles took a deep breath and turned to look out the window. "This guy's a tough nut, I don't know."

"He's a nut alright. But look at you. Mr. High School Hockey Star. Who was the high scorer on your team? You were. Don't let this clown stop you."

Charles set his plate down. He clenched a fist and began to punch it into his other hand.

Malloy pointed at him. "So quit talking like you're defeated."

The stare on Charles' face intensified. "I hope you're right."

"I know I'm right. Have I ever let you down?"

Malloy returned to his desk, scooped up a piece of pizza for himself, and dropped it onto a paper plate. He wiped his hand on a napkin and then slipped off the guitar strap. He set the guitar lovingly back onto its stand and returned to his desk.

"But listen. I've got some tv spots coming up in a month or two.

One of them shows me in some kind of an old style Western scene. They'll see me ride out in that sunset on their color t.v. screen, and like the song, I'm telling you, it'll be dynamite. I'm telling you things are going to just get better and better for us."

Chapter Twelve

That Sunday evening, Alex worked over his jigsaw puzzle at the card table in the kitchen, plugging in the final straight-edged pieces to complete the outer frame. There were sharp, black rocks at the bottom, blue waves on the sides and deep azure sky pieces across the top. He started to sort the remaining pieces by color. In the background, he heard his son David zoom a paper airplane around the living room with all sorts of rocket thruster noises added for extra effect.

Suddenly, Danielle jumped up, bumping her knee on the dining room table. "Not now David. Please. Go in the other room and play."

Alex heard David's plane whoosh into his bedroom and fade out. He watched as Danielle rose from the dining room table and crossed into the kitchen to pour herself some more coffee. For a moment, he followed her movements from the coffee maker to the dozen or so deep red beefsteak tomatoes lined up across the kitchen counter.

"Any luck with the job search?" He said.

"The job section is getting to be so…"

"Small?"

"Yes. Whaddya think? How fast do you think I could learn how to use a drill press?"

"I think you should look online."

"Only if you help me. I'm helpless online."

He stood up and gave her a hug. "You're not helpless in the garden."

She sprung free from his grip. "Not now. I'm not in the mood."

He watched her return to the dining room table and then flip the newspaper open to the used household items section. He tried to read her facial expressions, but she put on a poker face instead. After a minute, she slammed the paper shut.

"I suppose we should sell our crib now," she said.

"What? Why?"

"You know what the doctor said. Nothing seems to be working."

Alex sat down at the table opposite from where she was sitting. "I don't think it's hopeless, if that's what you mean."

"At least I can make veggies grow. Maybe I should start naming *them*."

Alex rolled his eyes.

"You're right. I suppose that'd make me a cannibal when I make salsa, huh?"

He glanced over into the living room to see a black, leather bound Bible laying on the coffee table.

"What?" She asked, cradling and sipping off of her purple coffee mug.

He pointed towards the living room. "Somebody left the Bible out."

Alex stood up and walked over to it. The cover was brand new, although he could see a bookmark jutting out of one of the pages. In that instant, a thought came to him.

Open the Word.

Alex glanced back at her, startled.

"What?" She said.

He opened the Bible up to a random page and read the first chapter number that he saw: Matthew, chapter 24. He slammed the cover shut and placed the Bible back onto the living room bookshelf.

"What was that all about?" She said.

"I was told to open the Word. So I opened the Word. Not sure what I was supposed to see."

Danielle pushed the classified section to the side and pulled out a Target ad. "Maybe we should have a garage sale. Baby stuff galore."

"Oh stop it. *I'm staying hopeful.*"

"Look. David's in school, I'm trying to go to work, and we're not having any luck with this. Maybe it's a sign. Doesn't the Bible talk about signs?"

"Sure. But it's not like you've had a vision or anything. Or like we've heard some booming voice saying 'Sellllll the crib! Sellllll the crib!'"

"That's not funny, Alex."

Danielle stood up and left the table, but this time Alex could see the anger in her features.

* * *

Two hours later, Alex lay in bed and stared at the window. He could not sleep, however, and the harder he tried the more his surroundings seemed to conspire against him. First, it was a car door slamming down the street. Then, it was the sounds of Danielle brushing her teeth in the bathroom. Then, there were headlights passing by on the bedroom window curtains. Finally, there came an internal restlessness that would not cease.

He let the minutes pass. He turned over and stared at the bright red numbers on their digital alarm clock. He rolled back towards the window again. The familiar rhythms of the night did nothing to sooth his unease. After he was sure Danielle was asleep, he sat up, and swung his legs over the edge of the bed. As peaceful as her presence normally was, the darkness that seemed to envelop his thoughts tonight would not let him keep his peace for long.

He stood up and stared down at his nightstand. He snapped up the brochure Kay gave him at the bookstore and meandered into the bathroom across the hallway. Closing the door behind him, he plundered the medicine cabinet for some Tylenol. He grabbed the bottle, pried off the cap, and tilted the bottle until two caplets tumbled out. He then filled up his water glass and downed the pills.

With a sigh, he sat on the edge of the bathtub and stretched out his legs. He unfolded the brochure and read the front flap. It quoted a verse from Matthew, chapter 24, referring to the signs of the End of an Age.

Inside the brochure it detailed what the acronym "LAMPS" stood for and listed their mission statement. It also commented how the physical printing, tracking, and safeguarding of coins and paper money could soon give way to an all-card orientated system that would be used in payphones, parking meters, vending machines, buses and taxis. Then, a dramatic shift would occur to move towards tracking chips inside of or on the back of a person's hand.

Alex rolled his eyes and rubbed his temples. Now he knew the real reason why Kay showed up at his door. The brochure went on to argue there would be no more line between the rich and the poor—in fact, it would be a line between the living and the dead. Grocery stores, banks, and movie theaters would all be forced onto this system. No mark? No sale.

He stood up and walked into the kitchen, stopping only a moment to dump the brochure into the bathroom trash can. In the kitchen, he pulled on the freezer door handle of the refrigerator and stuck his head inside.

Then came a whisper from behind him.

"Go to James and speak to him, for his deeds have come up before Me."

Alex straightened up and his eyes opened wide. He turned to look behind him. There was nothing to see except for his puzzle on the card table. It was a whisper unlike anything he ever heard, neither male or female.

He lurched towards the dining room and found nothing. He marched into the living room and circled back towards the bedroom hallway. Stealthily, he peered into the adjacent hallway and peered into David's room. "David?"

Silence.

"Alex?" Came his wife's voice a moment later. "Are you okay?"

He crept down the hallway again back towards the living room.

"Alex?"

On the dining room table he flipped open the A section of the Sunday newspaper and skimmed the headlines on each page.

It sure doesn't feel like the end times, he thought to himself.

In the paper, there was a story about a small earthquake in Indonesia. Trouble brewing in the housing market. A car bomb in Pakistan.

He shut the newspaper and frowned.

Oh whatever. Hasn't every generation felt at one point or another felt that they were in the end times?

He returned to bed.

"Alex?" Danielle said again.

"I'm fine. I just had a headache and took some Tylenol. Then I thought I heard a noise."

She held out an arm and he fell into it. She kissed him on the forehead, and then laid her head on his chest. The angst that swirled earlier in his mind now departed, although it was replaced by a vague sense of conviction. In minutes he was fast asleep.

Chapter Thirteen

For the rest of the week, Alex spent his lunch breaks at work hunkered down at his desk instead of hanging out in the break room or going out to eat. Early Thursday afternoon over his lunch, he sat at his desk and flipped open his Toshiba laptop that he brought from home. To the right of his laptop was a stack of printed articles Ian e-mailed him the day before. The top article was titled, "Local Mining Company Digs Out From Laptop Thefts".

To the left of his laptop, and in front of his Macintosh machine was a plate of food from a farewell potluck lunch for Lydia. He picked up a sample of everything from the folding table in the break room as not to offend anyone, and wondered if his stomach would fight back against an onslaught of coleslaw, barbecue meatballs, taco chips, spicy taco salad, spring rolls, lime gelatin, and dill pickle chips. He took a swig of Pepsi from his bright blue party cup and threw even more fuel on the proverbial fire.

He looked out towards the window one last time and steeled himself for what lay ahead. From behind his bunker of running computers and programming manuals, he felt ready for battle. He picked up the game disc that he received from Kay at the bookstore and slid it into his laptop's DVD drive. He crossed his arms and prepared himself to eject the disc and roll the system back if needed.

An introductory popup box came up on screen.

It appeared to be the standard end user license agreement, with the typical accept or decline buttons on the bottom. He scanned the entire text and looked for any weird clauses or political rhetoric.

With a few mouse clicks, he set the installation process in motion. He watched the computer screen a few minutes and toggled through several pages of installation configuration information. Another mouse click later, all the dialog boxes vanished and the screen filled with cartoon characters that were to lead him on an adventure in reading, science, and math.

Or so the back copy on the disc case read.

The adventure was based entirely in outer space, and involved the player taking a spaceship from planet to planet, galaxy to galaxy, on an interstellar knowledge hunt. He appreciated their efforts and instinctively knew that such a project must have taken hundreds of hours to plan, draw, assemble, and code. His own efforts at building games in the past were limited to Pac-Man clones and a decent knockoff of Breakout.

He played the game a few minutes, alternating between it and munching on his taco salad. At times the user interface hung, and in a few cases, he could see graphics artifacts and culling issues. He wrote these issues down on a legal tablet. When he reached a section called the "Fraction Factory" he decided to quit.

A message flashed across the screen and faded. It did not look like an error message dialog box that he was familiar with, because it was embedded in the main game window itself in a Comic Sans-type font.

Alex flipped to a new page on his legal tablet and attempted to write down what he witnessed. He tried backing up through several screens. Nothing unusual happened. Then, he ended and restarted the program. After the game restarted, he returned to the Fraction Factory and closed the game down again. Like before, a message flashed. He repeated the process ten more times until he caught every word and assembled the following phrase on paper:

DON'T TAKE THE MARK

He leaned back in his chair, confused. This would require further research, he figured. He copied every file off the compact disc onto his laptop hard drive and then ejected the disc. He put it back into its plastic case, handling it as if its edges could cut his fingers like the top of an opened can. He then scanned his laptop computer for viruses. Finding none, he sighed and stretched his arms.

He mused to himself about how fast Ian and him could have cracked such a game in their past days. With enough patience he figured he could probably reverse engineer large parts of the code, or at the least figure out what tools were used to build it.

Why am I thinking about that all of a sudden, he thought. He flipped back to the first page of his legal tablet and wrote down a list of five software bugs he noticed.

Lydia burst into his office seconds later, clutching her new cookbook. "Thanks, Alex."

He looked up, still lost in thought. After what seemed like a minute of silence, he said, "You're welcome."

Today she wore a vivid yellow and tangerine tie-dye tee shirt and jeans. If it was not her last day, he was sure Drew would have told her to go back home and tone down the volume of her outfit.

"Are they working you to death in here? You poor thing, you. What you need is a vacation. You want some of the vacation brochures I have in my desk? I have lots."

"No. I'll be out in a little bit."

"Liar."

"Serious. I will."

She gave an exaggerated head nod and left a second later.

He turned back to his laptop and slipped the game disc case back into his briefcase under his desk. Part of him wanted to completely blow the game installation away with a couple of commands, but another part of him knew another trip to Erin's Books would soon be in order.

* * *

An hour later, Alex was sitting in Charles' office, leaning back in a burgundy plastic and wire chair that looked like it came from the break room. His office was smaller than Drew's but more cluttered. On the walls were several sales appreciation plaques, a Minnesota Wild team poster, and a pair of high school hockey team photos with Charles in them. In the corner of his office, against a gray, steel filing cabinet, rested a taped-up wooden hockey stick with a pair of dusty black skates on the floor next to it.

On Charles' desk was a picture of his wife in a beautiful wedding gown, along with numerous pictures of their friends and some of his buddies. For all the pictures, however, Alex could only recall a conversation or two that involved his wife.

Alex stared on at a modified prototype of the Pegasus tracking bracelet, which Charles held now between his hands. The bracelet was painted bright neon green but the matchbook-sized, rectangular box that contained the tracking device was removed.

Charles gestured wildly with his hands. "Imagine this. You arrive at the mall. Let's say, the Mall of America. It's Christmas time, stores are packed, people are carrying packages, bags and boxes. Okay? Lines are long. You've got things to do at home, parties to go to, and your car is a hundred miles away in the back of a parking lot somewhere. What if you could just walk into the mall, and stop at an information booth by the door or a customer service desk and get a bracelet like this."

Alex sighed.

"Now, two things happen once you get this bracelet. First, it becomes a single source of cash and credit. You load the bracelet up with your credit information at the booth, and then you are free to travel about the mall. Second, it can be tracked by GPS if you choose. Know much about GPS?"

"A little. Basically, there are several satellites in orbit around the Earth, and you figure your location by trilateration. The GPS receiver tries to sync up with at least three of those satellites to figure out its position..."

"Okay. So, you're walking through the mall with your bracelet. You stop at a store. Get this—no need for cash, no need for a receipt."

"Wait. I don't know how well GPS works inside of big structures like a mall."

"Okay, then you get the mall to install a Wi-Fi system..."

"You're not listening. Wi-Fi has issues too. I mean, it's workable, but..."

"What's the other system then?"

"You mean Wi-Max? That relies on towers. Kind of like cell phones."

"Right."

"Wait. Why would you need GPS again?"

"To keep track of relatives. Kids. Teenagers. Everybody could split up, but still find each other."

"No. No GPS. Mobile phones sometimes do that already."

"Think. If we do this during the upcoming holiday season, people could get a temp ring at the door. Kind of like a promo. Then we stick some scanners in some stores. People leave and they turn in the bracelet and get a receipt. Piece of cake."

Alex folded his hands and leaned forward. He eyed the brass and wood sales appreciation plaques behind Charles on the walls. The plaques were a bit of a misnomer since their sales staff was so small. "Okay, let's say you cram sensors in the walls of the mall instead of GPS. Now what if someone steals your ring?"

"How could they? No one's gonna steal your ring. Maybe we could do some type of bionic scan."

"You mean biometric scan?"

"Yeah."

"No."

"Think Alex, this thing could cut down on bad checks being passed, too."

"It's funny you say that."

"What?"

"Somebody hit my account a few weeks ago, to the tune of several hundred dollars."

Charles shuffled through a set of papers on his desk. "Did you find out who did it?"

"No. Although I have a reasonable idea."

Charles cleared his throat and began to drum a pencil on his desk. "See, a system like this could eliminate that. The ring would work for you, and only you."

"I've never built a database or a tracking system like that."

"It's like a prison system. But a hundred times bigger."

"They're customers. Not convicts."

Charles threw his hands up in the air. "Geez, you're impossible to work with. Man, you're negative today."

"Besides, it'll cost too much."

"Negative, negative, negative."

"A mall would never approve of it because of the overhead. Do you know how many stores are in the Mall of America? I can't imagine the cost of all those scanners at the registers and then putting tracking devices in the walls. Where's the profit in that? Besides, how would you load up the bracelet with credit information? You'd have to bring your cards or cash to the mall, and then store them somewhere while you shop. Otherwise the ring would serve no purpose."

"Negative."

"Cut that out."

"Have the kids stash their valuables in the lockers by the doors. Valleyfair does that. Then you get a locker key. Or, maybe we could have it loaded up online. That'd be cool." Charles put his hands together and pointed at Alex. "We can make this happen. Don't. Think. Negative. You gotta have faith, man."

"Oh, I've got faith." Alex glanced towards the window and then the ceiling. "Well, most of the time I do."

"You know, you just need a cool codename for this."

"I dunno about that."

"Think of something."

"Pandora."

"Sounds like a metal band."

"Buckthorn."

Charles swore.

Alex zeroed in on a twisted tan rubber band sitting on the edge of Charles' desk. "How about Project Möbius?"

"Weird. Who's maybe-us?"

"It's a kind of ring."

Charles stared at him blankly.

"It's a math thing."

"Right. Okay. Maybe-us it is."

Alex stood up to leave while Charles continued.

"If the wristbands take off, we'll go bigger. Maybe something more personal. Better yet, implanted."

Alex felt his stomach begin to roll. The pickle chips and the soda suddenly seemed to come to a full boil. "What'd you just say?"

Charles leaned back and spread his arms wide with his palms facing upwards. "Don't start in on me."

"Does Aspirizon Bank have anything to do with this?"

"What? You're having one of your Jesus moments aren't you?"

"A Jesus moment?"

"Sure. Freaking out at the thought of new ideas that might shake up the norm."

Alex gave him a confused look. "You been talking to James Malloy or something? That's sounds like something he used to say."

"I don't know what you're talking about."

Alex stood up to leave. "I'll be in my office."

Chapter Fourteen

On Saturday Alex and Danielle spent the morning running errands. At one point, Alex directed her to pull into a strip mall parking lot, where Erin's Books was located. She parked the car but left the engine running. She glanced over in the direction of the bookstore and then looked back at Alex.

"What's over here?" She said.

From the glove compartment, Alex withdrew the compact disc Kay gave him a couple weeks before. "I'm here to return a highly confidential, top secret disc."

"Oh, right. Is that the game you played at work?"

"I played it on my lunch break."

"Riiiight."

Alex sat in the passenger seat a moment and pretended to read the back cover of the disc case again.

"Well, go on, Mr. Top Secret."

He stepped out of the car and into a brisk, warm breeze. The sun bore down on him, but in the wind, Alex felt October hiding. All the time he paced up to store, he kept thinking about the message flashing across his laptop screen.

When he entered the store, he discovered Kay sitting behind the counter with a man standing next to her. Both were going over a catalog of some sort.

"Interesting program you have here," Alex said, holding up the disc case.

"Did you like it?" Kay said, looking up from the counter.

"I'm not sure what to think." Alex then looked towards the man standing next to her. "Are you Kay's brother?"

"I am. Name's Brian." He extended a hand to shake. "Yours?"

"Alex. I…uh…took a keen interest in what you wrote here."

Brian stood there in a black and white striped tee shirt and blue jeans, with scraggly, shoulder length brown hair, a short beard and a mustache. He hooked his thumbs onto the belt loops of his jeans. Kay sat nearby on a barstool, wearing a pale yellow sweatshirt and black jeans.

Alex felt his shoulders tense up as he approached the counter. He set the disc in front of them. "It looks promising."

"Do you think it'll sell?" Brian asked with a genuine enthusiasm in his voice.

Alex flipped the disc case over on the counter. He examined every square inch of the counter but observed that the stack of compact discs that used to be next to the cash register was gone. He reached into his pants pocket and withdrew a folded-up piece of legal paper with a list of bugs on it. With steady hands he unfolded the paper and slid it towards Brian. "First, you have to fix these."

Brian scooped up the sheet and read it over. A smile came across his face. "Thanks, man."

"As for whether it will sell or not, well…I'm a little concerned about this logo on the back. What does it mean?"

Kay put her elbows on the counter and her chin on her folded hands. "It's the logo of our company. Not really a company. A side venture. Hopefully, we can…"

"No, I asked you, *what does it mean?"*

Brian cleared his throat. "It stands for truth. Or, light onto the truth."

"Truth? Hmmm. Let's see. It's a game that teaches fractions, a bit of algebra, some history, some science. Okay. Lots of truth there. Well done on the drawings by the way."

"Thanks," Kay replied, shifting her eyes to her brother and then back to Alex.

Alex turned to the side and leaned against the counter on one elbow. He glanced around at the store shelves and then back at Brian. "What about the messages I saw? They'd flash across the screen whenever I'd close it down."

"Messages?" Brian said.

"Messages. What does 'taking the mark' have to do with teaching a kid about the solar system?"

Kay stood up and crossed her arms. "What?"

"So would that be a feature or a bug?" Alex said.

Brian opened his mouth to speak but Alex put up a hand.

"Wait. Let me add to that. Where are you taking your cause? I read your brochure at home. The ones you keep behind the counter like a little, secret society. It preaches on and on about how financial tech as we know it is going to misused in the near future. Long on rhetoric, short on details."

Brian tried to continue. "First of all…"

Alex cut him off. "I look at your software and I look at your brochure and I don't know what to think. You argue about how we'll all be pulled into some massive system that we can never escape from once it's put in place. Fine. But don't stick it in your game. Keep the kids out of it. I copied your disc and everything on it, and so help me I better not find a virus on my system."

Brian held out his hands as if to try to calm Alex down. The gesture only startled Kay. "Look. Do you know what is happening around you? Right now, you have a choice on how to handle your money. You can write a check, use cash, use credit, whatever. But you know what?" He slammed his index finger down onto the counter. "Only one of those options is truly anonymous: *cash*."

"Okay."

"Oh, and look at this." Brian took out his wallet and pulled out several bills. "But there's a problem. Counterfeiting. Now we've started changing the colors of the bills."

"So?"

"What's next when that no longer works? Forced debit cards?"

Alex heard the tinkle of a small set of bells over the entry door of the store. He turned to see a mother of two with her children in tow enter the store.

Kay interrupted and put a hand on her brother's arm. "Keep it down. Customers are coming in."

Alex rolled his eyes. "That's years off. There's still some infrastructure to put into place. Look at vending machines."

"Oh, I don't know about that," Brian added. "Several countries are trying to become cashless societies. Countries in Europe are experimenting with all sorts of national databases as we speak. And then, you know what is next?"

Alex rubbed his temples. "Counterfeit cards?"

"Exactly. It's already happening." Brian lowered his voice and stared right through Alex. "And then along comes something really revolutionary—say, like an implanted chip."

He held up his left hand with his thumb and index finger an inch apart. "Some companies are already working on those. Think about it—it's original. Like fingerprints or the way your genetics are organized."

"There's ways around that."

"Oh, I dunno about that. Using cash, nobody knows who you are, except by relying on memory or maybe even a video store camera. Use a chip, and someone could always know how much money you have and where you are by tracking your purchases through it."

"The man's a walking brochure," Alex said, pointing his finger at Brian while looking at Kay.

Kay glanced at Alex.

Brian continued to raise his voice and swung his arms in the air. "Then, what if they go further and only allow certain people to receive or use the chip? What if that choice is based on your belief system? And if they don't like you…"

He snapped his fingers, startling Kay.

Alex smirked. "That's a lot of data to track. Terabytes worth. Petabytes, even. You're jumping to lots of conclusions, too."

"Sure, but tech's always improving. You know that. I'm sure you see it everyday."

"Well…"

"What's worse, though, is we gotta stop and think how we even got to this point. I mean, how much of the theft is artificially created? How much is *allowed* to happen in the first place?"

Alex backed away from the counter and stuffed his hands into his pockets. He cleared his throat and locked his eyes on the psychology section of the store. "My, uh, account just got hit a while back." He motioned towards Kay. "You know, not long after that, she came to my door."

Alex studied the reactions of Kay and Brian. Instead of distance, there was a look of genuine concern on both of their faces. The former anger in Brian's features eased back a bit, even though he crossed his arms.

"Alex, I had nothing to do with that," Kay said.

"You had my account info. Have anything else you forgot to give me?"

He eyed Kay as she looked around him to smile and wave at the mother and her children passing by.

"Do you shop online?" Brian asked.

"Rarely."

"Did you call the bank right away?"

"First thing I did."

"Which bank did you switch to?"

"That's none of your business."

Brian held up his hands again as if to calm the situation.

Kay walked out from behind the counter and walked into one of the aisles. She returned with a hardcover King James Version of the Bible and opened it up on the counter. She began leafing through its delicate gold-edged pages. "I was poring over my Bible last night, and I was thinking of you. I opened it up at random, and I came upon the Book of Jonah."

She glanced up at Alex.

Alex rolled his eyes and nodded his head. "I'm familiar with it."

"Isn't that the one where he gets swallowed by a whale?" Brian said.

"There's more to it than that. He was given a message by the Lord to go and speak to the Ninevites. There was evil in Nineveh at the time, but Jonah fled on a ship. Then the sea became rough all around the ship, and the sailors began praying to their individual gods. They cast lots, and it fell on Jonah. Eventually, they turned to him and he told them to throw him overboard."

Kay looked up as if to check Alex's reaction.

She turned the page and skimmed the text with her finger. "Then the sea calmed and Jonah was swallowed by a big fish. Three days later and after a prayer, he was spit out onto dry land. Again God spoke to him, and this time he listened. The city repented and was spared. God hasn't spoken to you lately, has he?"

"How big is your group anyway?" Alex barked back.

"Our group? You mean the software company?" Brian said.

Alex could feel his chest tightening up. "Right. Your group of activists."

"Activist is kind of a strong word, I think," Kay said.

"Whatever. I have to go."

Alex waved them off and headed towards the door. In the background, he could hear the mother and her two children shuffling up to the register while Kay and Brian argued quietly with one another.

* * *

Upon reaching the car, Danielle yelled at him through her open driver's side window. "What took you so long? Did ya get lost?"

Alex climbed back into the car and buckled his seatbelt.

"We argued about the game. And…they refused to listen."

Alex noticed Danielle staring hard at the bookstore. "I wish you would tell me what is on your mind more often."

"I do. I tell you everything."

Danielle began to drive off.

Alex sighed. "Does this have anything to do with the other night?"

"No. I had a headache the other night."

Danielle pouted, exaggerating her frown and scrunching her eyebrows at Alex.

"I know. I shouldn't bring my work home with me."

As she pulled out onto the highway, he studied the side streets, the cars in the other lane, and the billboards on the side of the road. Then, he saw another Liberty Card billboard with the eerie colors and the woman with the magnetic eyes.

"Not again," he said all of sudden.

"What?"

"Don't you see it? The stupid billboards are everywhere."

"So?"

"They're creepy, Danielle."

"You really do need a vacation."

"No, seriously."

"I think the cards are cool."

"Oh no. Not you, too."

"What are you talking about?" She reached over to feel his forehead with the back of her hand.

He maneuvered the seat into a reclined position and closed his eyes. At least that way he didn't have to deal with anything.

"Danielle, people are getting their accounts hit left and right. And then they're flocking to that stupid thing as if it will save them somehow."

"This is really bugging you isn't it?"

"Lot of things bug me. This is a special kind of bug. By the way, whaddya know about the Book of Jonah?"

"Let's see. There's a whale. And then there's a naughty prophet. Oh, and a ship I think. Do I win something?"

"No, but the lady in the store kept going on about Jonah."

"This is the same one that dropped off your papers? Weird."

"That's what I thought."

Chapter Fifteen

Three days later, James Malloy reclined in his desk chair, staring at baseball scores on his computer monitor. His beloved Cubs swept the Pirates days earlier and were now playing the Florida Marlins while fighting off the Brewers for sole possession of first place.

He then switched over to a covert application that monitored basic, worldwide usage statistics of a music file and playlist sharing program called Seagle. He admired the black, white, and sky blue seagull logo a moment on the application interface. The software was installed on thousands of machines across the planet, and freely available on the web. Each instance of Seagle, however, was also capable of contacting one of several servers. The software plus the server network allowed everything to work in concert with one another to form a symphony of sorts.

A symphony of destruction, to be exact.

Suddenly, the telephone rang, breaking his concentration. At first he did not want to answer. He stared at the caller identification display on his phone. It was his wife.

"How late are you going to be tonight?" She said, sounding cranky.

"I'm going to be stuck here for another couple of hours. Don't hold up dinner for me."

"Have you seen the news?"

"Anne, I don't have a television set up here."

"One of the bank branches is burning. It's all over the news. It's in Plymouth!"

A wry smile broke across his face. Ben really was reliable after all. He tried to sound incredulous, and stood up from his desk chair. "Really? I wonder if I can see it from here."

He reached into his desk and pulled out his Bushnell binoculars. He set down the phone receiver and went up to a window and glassed the skyline to the northwest. There, in the distance, sure enough, he could see a small plume of black smoke against the backdrop of a sunset. It was quite a little show despite it only being seven o'clock in the evening.

He returned to his desk and picked up the phone. "It's quite a sight. I better call the branch manager to check on him."

"Jim, please come home."

"I can't. I have too much…"

"I don't care."

"The shareholders care."

He heard her rattle off a string of expletives and so he held the phone a few inches away from his ear. When she stopped yelling, he took a deep breath and replied. "Anne, stop it. You know it breaks my heart to see you getting yourself all worked up. The doctor warned you about this. Turn off the tv and do something for yourself. There's some gin in the cupboard…"

"I don't want any…"

He held the phone away from his ear again as she let another barrage of expletives fly.

"Anne, go to bed."

She went quiet for a minute.

"Anne?"

"Please Jim. Come home."

"Alright. I'll try to hurry. Good night, Anne."

He hung up the phone and got up from his desk. He wandered over to his guitar stand and picked up his old friend. He struck a pose like the guitarist on the poster on the wall behind him. This moment called for a celebration. He relished the thought of boxes of evidence and annoying legal paperwork being consumed by the flames, almost to the point of wishing he could have lit the initial match himself.

As he slipped the guitar strap over his shoulder, he walked over to the window again and eyed the plume of smoke. He admired its darkness. What was it his father used to say? Oh yes. "They will be called oaks of righteousness, a planting of the Lord."

He chuckled to himself and strummed out the opening notes of *The Trees*. He then began to sing the first line of the song.

A second later he heard the security doors click behind him. He turned to see Susan walk in carrying a stapled, brown paper bag full of Chinese food from a restaurant down the block. "What timing," he said with a smile.

"Hope you're hungry. They gave me gobs of rice."

"Did I ever tell you, you look amazing today?"

Susan blushed and set the bag down on the corner of his desk next to the jar of cinnamon bears. She brushed her platinum blonde bangs back out of her eyes. Tonight she wore a white and powder blue patterned sweater, more suitable for late fall or winter rather than late summer.

"Thanks," she said after opening up a box of steaming Kung Pao chicken.

Malloy glanced back at the smoke and noticed the moon was rising just above the horizon. He strummed out a different song on his guitar and began to sing the opening lines of *Moondance* to her.

Susan turned to look back at Malloy. "Are you trying to serenade me?"

He stopped playing and walked over to his desk. "Maybe."

She scooped out some of the Kung Pao chicken onto a paper plate and then opened a box of white rice. She looked over his shoulder and towards the window. "Wow. What is that?"

"What?"

"Smoke. There's smoke over there."

She wandered over to the window and crossed her arms. James turned his attention to opening a packet of soy sauce.

"What's burning?"

"One of our branches."

"What? Shouldn't you go down there?"

"Nah. I'd get in the way. It's late, the place is empty and the branch manager is on vacation."

"What branch is it?"

"It's one of the ones in Plymouth."

"Is that the one we were going to close down next month?"

"Technically, it's already closed, dear. Besides we had to get rid of some paperwork. You know, some lawsuit and accounting related garbage."

"James, what did you just do?"

He smiled and sprinkled soy sauce on his rice. Then he dug into the rice on his plate. "I didn't do anything."

She crossed her arms and stared on at the smoke.

The telephone rang again. Malloy looked down at the phone. He reached down and grabbed a hold of the telephone cord and unplugged it from the wall. Then he continued to enjoy his meal.

"Shouldn't you answer that? I'll get it."

"No, don't worry."

A moment later, his cell phone began to ring. He quickly switched it off.

"Who was it?" Susan asked. "It might be about the fire."

"I think it's a telemarketer."

"What if it's your wife?"

Malloy set his plate down on his desk and popped open a can of Pepsi.

"You mean my soon-to-be ex-wife, right? Those divorce papers just can't move through the courts fast enough."

Truth was, he reflected, there were no divorce papers and his wedding ring was sitting inside his briefcase. *Why complicate things now?*

* * *

At first, Alex found himself standing on a dirt road running through an abandoned desert town. In the distance beyond the trees were sandstone cliffs, rusty brown and looming, yet unreachable. The dirt road stood empty, and the windows of the town's shops hid behind weathered boards and sheets of plywood. Tumbleweeds, stirring, prowled the streets.

A russet-colored sign hanging in front of one of the buildings read: "General Merchandise" and next to the entrance was a wooden post for tying up horses, although no horses could be found. The sun bore down on his neck, the heat of the road came up through his shoes, and the sky, tinged with dust, offered no clouds.

On the edge of the town, towards the cliffs, he noticed three men crouched over a figure lying face down on the ground. As he walked towards them, they did not notice his approach. The three figures wore bandanas around their foreheads and one of the men bent down over a businessman in the road, who was wearing a dirtied white dress shirt and navy blue dress pants. He did not recognize the faces of the men, but one of them now withdrew a switchblade from his front pants pocket and stabbed it into the businessman's right hand, cutting crude, jagged strokes that drew pools of blood. The blood plopped onto the dust now, but Alex could not speak.

"There it is," the man with the knife said, holding up a bloodied, dime-sized disc with his thumb and forefinger. "Isn't it beautiful?"

Then, Alex heard someone shouting, then running and then footsteps pounding down the street behind him. The three men fled, dropping the switchblade into the dirt. Alex reached the businessman, and bent over him. The man's left hand still clenched an open briefcase with its contents askew and vulnerable to the wind. As he turned over his lifeless body, he recognized it was Drew Arthur.

Seconds later came darkness. Although Alex thought he opened his eyes, waving his hand in front of his face did nothing. He reached down with his hands. His palms touched a floor of some sort, which was cold and flat, but pitted, as if made of concrete. He reached in front of him and sensed nothing. He reached up with one hand, but found no ceiling, making the only sure thing the floor. He stutter-stepped forward, inching his way towards something.

Anything.

He shouted.

Echoes replied.

He hollered again.

The echoes screamed back.

Then, a tiny point of light in the distance drew him forward. Step by tiny step, heartbeat by stifling heartbeat, he crept towards an answer.

The point of light seemed to shrink back with every advance he made. Alex's left hand abruptly hit something hard, smooth, and vertical. It was a wall, pitted again like concrete, cold like a snow bank. His right hand found it, too, and together they moved up, left, right, down and up again until he reached for the light, which turned out to be a star amongst many. Framed by a window, the stars were blocked in places by four vertical, probably iron, bars only inches apart.

He pressed his face to the bars and saw the moon beginning to rise over the horizon, creating spindly silhouettes out of a nearby set of woods. His right hand at this time began to throb, and as he held it up he noticed it was wrapped in gauze bandages. Frantically, he tore them off.

He turned his right hand towards the light. Next to a surgical incision, he saw a disc—dime-sized and black as the sky. Flicking his hand, he looked at it again, and the disc fell to the floor and the incision was gone.

* * *

Seconds later, he awoke, wrapped in thick blankets. He was sweating, overheated, yet truly awake. Shaken, he swung his legs over the end of his bed and wiped the sweat off of his forehead with his hand. The gray tee shirt he wore to bed was soaked now, front and back. He stood up, and meandered towards the closet. He found a new shirt and staggered down the hallway and into the kitchen. He changed his shirt and ran a hand through his ruffled hair.

"Go to James," he mocked to himself silently. He glared towards the ceiling. A wave of doubt about Kay and Brian blindsided him, as he opened the doors of the cupboard over the stove. Tossing aside a box of pancake mix and a bag of wild rice, he looked for an electronic bug of some sort or even a speaker. Was the voice he heard the other week even real? He scanned the cupboards one by one.

Then he peered over at the jigsaw puzzle on the card table with its outline of an ocean scene. A pile of unplaced pieces still lay beside the outer frame of the puzzle. He felt an urge to flip the table over for some reason.

"Alex, are you okay?" Came his wife's harsh whisper from the bedroom.

"I'm fine. Just a nightmare."

He pulled out a black coffee mug from the cupboard and filled it with water from the sink. He waited a minute in silence, then opened up her white leather purse. He dug around for her wallet and flipped through the assorted cards inside. When he found her Abernathy's shoppers card, he went over to the block of kitchen knives on the counter and pulled out the black-handled kitchen shears.

Without thinking, he clipped her card in half and tossed it into the garbage. In haste, he put the shears back and hurried into the living room.

From the bookcase, he withdrew the Bible and set it on the dining room table. He put his thumb between the pages of the Old Testament and flipped it open with abandon. His eyes fell on the following line: "But Jonah ran away from the Lord and headed for Tarshish. He went down to Joppa…"

He slammed the cover shut and sprang up from the table in disgust. As he slipped the Bible back into the bookcase, he heard Danielle wander down the hallway and into the kitchen.

He stood up and greeted her. "Sorry."

She wore a dark blue silk nightgown and shuffled towards him wearing yellow-duck slippers. She squinted and put a soothing hand up to his forehead. "You're burning up. Maybe you should call in sick."

Alex sighed and they returned to bed. For a half hour he stared at the wall and thought about how his workload would only increase in the weeks leading up to Thanksgiving. As much as he wanted a vacation right now, he knew the hours spent at work were about to get longer.

Chapter Sixteen

As September faded, October arrived in gusts, knocking the fire and rust from the trees. Alex sat in his office with his door closed and pored over two sets of database specifications: one for Pegasus and the other for Möbius. He looked up at the wall clock, which read 5:30 in the evening, and then peered out from behind his computer monitor towards the window. The sky remained dark, overcast and rainy, which helped him to concentrate more on his work to some extent.

He glanced back down at his desk and then over at his briefcase which sat on the floor next to him. His desk was covered in a sea of specifications, schematics, and open manuals. Somewhere, under the ocean of documentation, a manila envelope full of newspaper clippings from Ian remained submerged. Earlier in the day he rummaged through the envelope to find some notes about Abernathy's shopper cards. In his mind, he felt even more justified for cutting Danielle's card in half last week considering what he read.

Through the walls he could hear arguing and a fist pounding a desk. It was followed moments later by a yelling and a slamming down of a phone receiver. Alex perked up and waited, knowing most of the sounds were likely coming from Charles' office. Then came more yelling.

"What is with you guys? How hard can it be to make a prototype? I was watching a documentary last night. About how stadiums are built. Those guys put up the Skydome faster than you guys worked," A voice said through the walls.

Alex jumped up and bolted to his door. He opened it a crack but remained behind it to listen.

"We're working on it. I gave you the latest specs this morning," said Raj Sjidjar, a junior software engineer.

"Yeah, yeah. Can't you guys come in on Saturday for a few hours? C'mon. Let's push through this."

Alex opened his door all the way and then stepped into Charles' office, cradling a coffee mug. "Is there a problem?"

"Yeah, there's a problem. I'm losing contracts. Can't you guys come in on the weekend?"

"You don't. Why should we? Raj, go home."

Raj left the office shaking his head.

Alex leaned against the doorframe and looked over at Charles' desk. The desk seemed to be covered in waves of paperwork. "Just because Drew's out of the office for a couple days doesn't make you the boss by default," he said.

Charles peered out from behind his monitor and put his hands behind his head. Then he said, "Just because you're the teacher's pet doesn't make you the one with all the answers."

"Oh, give it up."

"At least I'm not paranoid like you are."

"What are you talking about?"

"You're stalling on the maybe-us project. I can see it."

"Who's stalling? Go look at my desk!"

For the first time, Alex noticed a new darkness to Charles' complexion. It was as if a shadow passed over his features.

"Ever since I mentioned implanted chips you've been weirding out on me," Charles snapped.

"It's a weird idea."

"I don't care about all that."

"You should."

"I don't."

Just then, Alex's desk phone rang. He charged out of the office and caught his own phone on the third ring. It was Danielle. He scooped up a pen off his desk.

"And I thought of something else for your list. I'm mastering the art of list making today, I swear," she said happily. "Wait. Did you grab my shopper's card?"

Alex let out a deep sigh. "No. I cut it up."

"What? Why?"

He tried to dig around for the manila envelope from Ian. An assembly language manual slammed to the floor with a bang. "I've been doing some reading. I'll explain later. We shouldn't shop there anymore, though. There's a new grocery store that opened up across town and..."

"Alex, that card saves us money. Why on earth..."

"Listen, I have to go, okay? It's so busy here, but I'll be home soon. Promise."

"You said that last Friday. You missed half of David's play."

"I know. I'm sorry. I said that Friday and said it again this morning. I tried to take the day off, but..."

"Don't apologize to me. Apologize to him."

"I did."

"When?"

"Friday night and this morning. All weekend. I dunno. Listen, I'll get everything on the list, okay? Bye." As he hung up the phone he leaned back in his chair and stared blankly at the walls.

* * *

Alex pulled into his garage three hours later and sensed something was wrong. He struggled to keep his eyes open despite downing a large cup of French Roast from Caribou Coffee a half hour earlier. Nevertheless, he pushed his body past the exhaustion point and got out of his car. He unloaded two bags of groceries from the trunk and headed inside.

Oblivious to the time, he clomped his way upstairs and set the bags down on the kitchen counter. He heard a rustling noise in the living room but tried to ignore it. Danielle entered the kitchen a moment later, half asleep and yawning. She stood in the doorway with her arms crossed. "What took you so long?"

"I stopped at the store."

She shuffled over to the counter and peeked into the one of the grocery bags on the counter. "Did you buy paper towels?"

"Yes."

"Aspirin?"

"Yes."

"How about throat drops?"

Alex cringed and closed his eyes as he set a carton of eggs into the refrigerator. "No."

"Did you write a list?"

"Yes."

"What did you do with it?"

He felt his cheeks become flush as he pulled out an ice-cold jug of milk. "I forgot it at work. But I'll go to the corner store after I put the rest of the food away. I bought some frozen juice bars."

She paced over to the freezer and tore open the box of bars. A slam of the freezer door later she headed into David's bedroom. "And tomorrow, you can get me a new shopping card. Thanks."

Alex drew a deep breath and finished emptying out the grocery bags. After folding up the bags and putting them in the broom closet next to the refrigerator, he leaned against the kitchen counter and stared at the floor. It needed sweeping.

In minutes Danielle reentered the living room and picked up her pillow from the sofa. With a mixture of irritation and sadness he watched her march towards their bedroom. He meandered into the living room and noticed a newspaper opened up to an article with pictures of a building fire. His eyes zeroed in on the headline: "Arson suspected in bank blaze".

"What is it?" She said.

He could see a weary disappointment in her eyes. "When did this happen?"

"The other night. It was all over the news."

"I didn't hear about it."

She turned away.

"Isn't this where you were the other day?" He said.

She stopped midway down the hallway. "Yeah."

"Why didn't you say something?"

"You were too busy."

"Sorry. I didn't realize…"

"It's okay. It's not like I escaped through the flames or anything."

Alex set the paper down and walked down the stairs that led to the garage. His heart grew heavy. His shoes felt like concrete blocks. Then, as he grasped the ice-cold doorknob of the garage service door, she called out to him.

"Forget the store. You're tired."

With a sigh of relief, he nodded and turned back around. In minutes he was sure that once his head hit the pillow he would be fast asleep.

* * *

Ben sat in the chair against the mirrored wall of the pool hall, staring blankly out across the floor. The lighting in the pool hall was dim at best, except for the white discs cast down from the bank of lights above each table. Ben scanned the crowd and counted four empty tables. He then analyzed the incoming crowd by the front door—nothing but a bunch of teenagers trying to impress one another. In the background, eighties hard rock music played, punctuated by the crack of eight and nine-ball breaks and the sound of wooden racks being set onto the table felt.

He then turned his attention to his friend Sean Oliver, who loomed over the table now. Sean stood five-foot four, and looked as if he had not eaten in a week. He had brutally short, rust-colored hair and sunken eyes as if he missed a day of sleep on purpose. He wore a black and white checkered flannel shirt over a white tee shirt with a worn out pair of jeans.

"Seven, corner pocket," Sean called out, pointing in Ben's direction.

He then watched Sean send the seven ball rocketing into the corner.

"Eight, side pocket."

Ben looked down at his cell phone and noticed a new text message. He brought it up onscreen. It was from James Malloy.

Congratulations on a job well done. But I have another favor to ask.

Ben texted him back. *Why?*

Just one more favor.

Ben glanced up to see the cue ball pop the eight ball off the table and into the wall. To him Sean looked strung out on something, although he could not figure out what. He scooped up the eight ball and set it back onto the felt and texted Malloy back.

No.

One more favor.

We had a deal.

I need an answer...

Ben shook his head and slapped the cover shut on his phone. He turned to Sean and said, "Whatta moron."

Ben stood up and rolled the eight ball into position. With a look of confidence, he parked the cue ball behind it, but suddenly hesitated a moment.

He bent down and aimed at the eight ball, but then backed off. He walked over to the right side of the table and again measured his shot. The angles were not ideal, he reasoned, so he walked around to opposite side of the table.

"Just shoot already, will ya?" Sean said. To Ben, his voice sounded like a creaky wooden door.

Ben then returned to his original position and measured his shot yet again, as if he was mixing and measuring chemicals in a lab. He lightly tapped the eight ball into the side pocket. "You know what this here game reminds me of?"

"What?"

"It reminds me of a video I saw once about fission. A neutron hits a uranium-235 nucleus and splits it. That sends more neutrons into other atoms and it goes on and on."

Ben then lined up for his final shot on the nine ball. "Nine ball, corner pocket," he said. "In the video, they show a room full of mousetraps with ping-pong balls on 'em. Ya hit one trap with a ball and the whole room goes off."

"Ya lost me."

"Aw, yaur always lost."

With a sharp pop he slammed the nine ball into the corner pocket. To him, pool was becoming as easy as the mechanics of fission.

Sean already turned his attention to one of the television sets in the corner of the pool hall. Ben watched, too, as he saw James Malloy ride out into the sunset on a horse, complete with a goofy cowboy hat, in an ad for Aspirizon Bank.

Next came a news story about the recent Aspirizon Bank blaze. Ben took a deep breath. They showed James Malloy standing out in front of the smoke-and-water-damaged blackened ruins of the bank.

"It's certainly a tragedy," Malloy said. "But thankfully no one was here at the time. We got a relocation plan in place for the employees. It breaks my heart to see good people suffer."

Ben pulled out the rack for another game of nine ball, even though technically Sean should have done that. "Whatta moron," he mumbled under his breath as he corralled the billiard balls into the wooden rack. He looked up at the television screen. "Whatta moron."

Chapter Seventeen

The inside of Ol' Mexico Restaurant always struck Alex as looking a bit like the inside of a cathedral. From the two-story high vaulted ceiling, to the arch-like stained glass windows with roses on them, to the extensive brickwork around the interior, Alex remembered this place well from when he ate there as a teenager with his parents. Complete with a gurgling fountain in the middle of one section of the restaurant, he sometimes felt as if it were a sanctuary of sorts, especially on a cold Minnesota winter night.

Tonight, the restaurant was half-filled with customers, with some of the faithful watching the New England Patriots taking on the Cincinnati Bengals on Monday Night Football, and some just coming in to escape the cold, early October rain and lightning storm outside. Rain had been pouring for at least an hour, and Alex was sure the remnants of Danielle's garden at home would be flooded by now.

Alex and Ian sat in a booth, munching on warm tortilla chips out of a wooden basket on the edge of the table. Moments earlier, their waitress dropped off a Numero Tres combination of three cheese enchiladas for Ian and a Numero Dos combination of a shredded beef taco, a tostada, and a cheese enchilada for Alex.

Ian dug his fork into an enchilada. "Did you ever find the guy that messed up your account?"

"Nope. After you sent me those photos, the trail went cold."

Ian leaned back a moment and took a long pull off his strawberry margarita. "Okay. Here's something I found out. Remember those laptops we talked about?"

"The Toshiba Satellites?"

"Sounds like a band name. Anyway, you didn't hear this from me. I was checking out some carders forums and it turns out lots of laptops were stolen over the past year. Then they started getting dumped off in odd places."

"Like?"

"Restaurants. Libraries. Parks. Now, here's the kicker." Ian paused a moment to savor a bite of his enchilada. "Only a handful of the hot accounts were Aspirizon accounts."

"Meaning what?"

"Meaning I bet someone's trying to drive business to the bank."

Alex leaned forward and took a sip off of his glass of ice water.

Ian set his fork down. "And…remember the branch that went up in smoke? Seems like they found something goofy in the pond out on the front lawn. Some lady said in the paper it looked like the whole pond burst into flame before the building went up."

"How does a pond burn?"

"Don't know."

Just then another bolt of lightning struck across the street. The windows rattled even above the sound of the Mexican music playing over the restaurant's sound system. Alex noticed a police car zipping by on the road out in front of the restaurant a moment later.

"What I wanna know is, how did the account numbers get on the laptops?" Ian said.

"Good question. Hey, did I ever tell you about our Möbius project at work?"

"No."

"It's a retail version of our prison bracelet system. One of our sales guys mentioned a potential customer. Guess who."

"If you say my ex-girlfriend, dinner's on you."

Alex rolled his eyes. "Jimmy Malloy."

Ian looked confused and took another sip of his drink as if it would help somehow. "Sounds like a comedian."

"Jimmy. No, no. Ol' Slyhand Malloy's no comic. Quick with a pick and quicker to pick your pocket."

"I don't get it."

"He's the president of Aspirizon Bank."

"Ooooh. That's bad."

"I'm wondering if I even want to make this system. I sure don't feel like spending the rest of my days securing the dumb thing."

"If you do keep going with it, lemme know when you go live with it. I wanna corner the market on aluminum foil."

Alex shook his head and took a drink off his water glass. "I mean it. This isn't fun anymore. Remember the games we used to look at?"

"Like yesterday. Trade you a Lode Runner for a Swashbuckler."

"Remember all the copy programs? Then copy protection. Sector gaps, skewed tracks…"

"Custom OSs, product activation, DRM…"

"We both know nothing's hackerproof. I tried telling that to the sales guy. He didn't get it. I mean, imagine a big one-stop shopping network of rings. It would be field day for a thief."

Ian flagged down their waitress and pointed his fork at Alex. "Mr. IT prophet, just trust us."

"No really, Mr. Marketer, it's true."

Alex finished off his Spanish rice and scanned the restaurant, lost in thought.

"Maybe you need to get out of there," Ian said, downing the last of his drink.

Ian reached over to the wooden basket of tortilla chips at the edge of the table. The basket was lined with paper and half full of chips. He dunked one in salsa and held it up in the air. "Better yet, you need an invention of your own. Did I ever tell you the story of Monster Crunchers?"

"What's that?"

"I read about it in a trade magazine once. I couldn't wait to get my hands on a box. They were corn chips made into all sorts of cool shapes. Miniature cars, planes, boats, helicopters, heck, even buildings."

Now Alex gave Ian a confused look.

"Serious business. The box had a picture of a Godzilla-monster thing on the front. It was demolishing buildings and eating cars."

"And what happened?"

"I don't know. We're carried 'em for about a month. Then some lady flipped out and complained that it caused her kid to start sticking real Matchbox cars in his mouth. I guess he broke a tooth or something. We had to pull the whole line."

Alex gave him a half-smirk.

"True story." Ian pointed to his own chest. "I bought a dozen boxes myself."

"Am I supposed to be inspired by that?"

"My point is that all it takes is a great idea."

Alex stared up at the television in the corner behind Ian.

"Maybe what you really need to do is to delegate," Ian said.

"To who? We're overloaded as it is and not hiring. No, what's really getting to me are the fights."

Ian scrunched his eyebrows, confused.

"Everything with Danielle is turning into a fight now. What I miss at the store, how late I work, how I park the car. I'm so tired. I can't keep track of time sometimes. I've had dreams so real I thought the next day it was part of reality. Probably didn't help that I cut up her shoppers card."

"No. Not her Abernathy's card."

"Yeah, I did it."

"I'm going to have to report you now to upper management. Maybe you can cut back on your hours."

"I tried changing my hours. I fell behind. Sometimes it's easier to work instead of fight, you know what I mean?"

Alex leaned back in his seat and stared on at the television in the corner again. "Oh no," he said suddenly.

"What?"

Ian turned around to watch the television himself. There, up on the screen, was the latest ad for Aspirizon Bank. It showed a cloud of dust approaching the viewer and suddenly a man on horseback appeared and turned his horse sideways to talk to the camera. Neither one of them could understand what he was saying over the murmur of the crowd.

Alex squinted and could see it was James Malloy onscreen. "Looks like Malloy. Can you read lips?" He asked Ian.

Ian paused a minute.

"I think he said something about being Dudley Do-Right. I don't buy it. Maybe Snidely Whiplash or something…"

A moment later their waitress arrived. She was a cheerful woman with curly, jet black hair, a petite stature and an olive complexion. She carried herself with a confidence that made Alex think she could knock a chip off any guy's shoulder.

She picked up an empty appetizer plate near Alex.

"Could I get a glass of water?" Ian asked.

"Sure thing."

The ad on the television came to an end with the words "Liberty

Cards" blazing across the screen.

"Ugh," Alex said.

"What? The guy in the ad?" She said.

"Yeah."

"I think he's kind of cute."

Alex groaned. "Not you too." He shook his head.

The waitress gave a huge smile, dropped off their individual checks and left the table.

"Isn't there anybody in this town that sees what's going on?" Alex said, staring at his bill.

* * *

By the time Alex left the restaurant, the rain fell even harder. On the way home he dodged so many huge puddles on the freeway that he felt like he was a boy again playing Monaco GP in the arcade. His windshield wipers batted furiously against the rain. More than once he was forced to slow down to avoid hydroplaning. He left his car radio off too, preferring the predictable rhythms of the wipers and the rain.

As he pulled into his driveway, he thumbed the button on the garage door opener.

Nothing happened.

He hit the button five more times, aiming the control in several different directions. On the seventh try, the garage door opened halfway and then stopped. He pushed the button again and the door went back down. Two more button presses and the door finally went completely up. He parked his car and pushed the button once, and of course, this time it worked.

Once inside the house, he padded up the stairs softly and walked into the bathroom. He flipped on the light and ran a hand through his disheveled hair. His face looked pale in the mirror and his eyes were developing dark marks underneath. His shoulders slumped as he brushed his teeth and then went to bed.

He snuck into the bedroom. In the closet, he dug out a tee shirt and a pair of sweats. Behind him he heard Danielle stir and when he turned around he noticed she was staring, concerned, at him. He sat on the edge of the bed as she reached out and felt his cheek. Then she closed her eyes.

"I love you," he whispered.

"I love you, too."

He changed out of his work clothes and slipped on the tee shirt and sweats. The ensuing silence worried him, however. Rain trickled down the bedroom window.

"The dishwasher is broken. And David needs help with Mrs. Delaney," Danielle said in a soft voice above the rain.

"His Kindergarten teacher?"

"Yes. She's singling him out for a lot of things and he's getting in trouble for things he is not even involved with. I need you to talk to her if you can tomorrow."

"Got it."

"And the garage door has been acting up."

"I noticed."

A flash of lightning lit up the bedroom curtains, but there was no thunder.

Alex lay on his side for a good twenty minutes following their conversation. He tried to let the rhythm of the falling rain, the peaceful sound of Danielle's breathing, and his own physical exhaustion carry him off to sleep. His mind, though, reeled with the possibilities of abandoned laptops sitting in service stations and restaurants throughout the country.

I'm not going to Malloy, Lord, he thought to himself. *I have got a past. You forgive, but he doesn't.*

Chapter Eighteen

A few days later on Friday evening, Ben sat alone in a booth at a Perkins restaurant near Erin's Books, and waited for his food to arrive. The restaurant was still half full, despite it being eight in the evening. He studied the tables around him, always observing, but never letting his eyes rest on any one table or any one person too long. He half wondered if anybody in the restaurant ever visited the bank he torched.

He withdrew a blue-and-white packet of sugar from the white plastic holder on the table and examined it closely. On the edge of the packet, he spied a tiny brown stain and thus set the packet aside. He selected another packet, turned it over in his fingers, and set it aside, too. After examining six separate packets for flaws, he tore open the last packet in the holder and emptied it into his steaming coffee.

He then studied the single-serving half-and-half containers in the ceramic white dish next to the sugar holder. Again, he picked over the containers until he found the perfect one. He poured it slowly into his cup.

With a spoon he swirled the creamer and sugar together in the coffee, staring at them as if watching rotating clouds in the sky. Sucrose, he knew, decomposed into caramel under intense heat, but more importantly, when combusted, turned into water, carbon and carbon dioxide. When mixed with potassium nitrate it became something a little more special. It became something known to amateur rocket hobbyists as rocket candy.

In other words, it became perfect for burning.

He flipped open his daily newspaper that he brought with him, but found himself drawn to a conversation going on behind his booth. He overheard a man and a woman discussing technology of some sort.

"I've been doing some digging on that Alex guy. That one that showed up at the bookstore," the man said.

"And?" The woman replied.

"I found out he works at a company called Hoyle-Aspen. They make tracking bracelets for prisons, house arrest systems and all that."

"Okay. But I could have told you that weeks ago, Brian."

"I also found his name on a whitepaper case study for a jail in southeastern Wisconsin. Turns out their rings could eventually be used there. The rings are traceable…get this…for miles."

"You seem appalled by that."

Ben cleared his throat, but continued to pretend to read his newspaper. As he read, his left hand began to fidget with his fork, rolling it over and over again in its napkin.

The man behind him spoke up again, but lowered his voice.

"Okay, but remember what I told you about the bank?"

The woman whispered now, too. "Aspirizon?"

"Yep. I found another whitepaper case study out there about using a similar ring in retail. Guess whose name I found in the small print as a sponsor." The man paused a moment. "*The bank.*"

"Oh, how curious."

Ben looked up from his newspaper and turned around to see the back of the head of a long-haired man taking a sip off his coffee and wearing a faded jean jacket. Across from him was a woman with reddish-brown, shoulder-length hair, and intense eyes. She wore narrow oval eyeglasses and a celery green sweatshirt. The woman turned to the side a moment to watch someone coming in the door of the restaurant. It was then Ben noticed a row of tiny silver hoop earrings on one of her ears. He figured maybe she had a bit of a rebellious streak in her and found himself remotely attracted to her.

"Sorry," Ben said. "I…uh…don't mean to eavesdrop, but I heard something about prisons and testing. Happen to know where?"

The man turned around to look at him and the woman stared at him, too. "They're in Wisconsin," the man said. "Walworth prison, I think. Why?"

"Seriously? I know someone there. What do these rings do?"

"Track you for miles if you escape. It's pretty effective. Blows the current systems out of the water. Know anything about tech?"

"A little." Ben extended a hand to the man to shake. "Name's Ben."

"I'm Brian," the man said.

The woman at the table extended her hand to shake. "And I'm Kay."

"Where do y'all learn all this stuff?"

Kay spoke up. "We both do a lot of research."

Kay reached into her jacket pocket and extended a brochure to Ben. "Here. Take one of these. Read up and learn. May I ask how long your friend is in for?"

"A few months." Ben took the brochure and skimmed its contents. "Says here you guys have meetings."

"Monthly. Care to join?" Kay laughed a bit, but Brian stayed serious.

"I could check ya out."

"We're going to have one tomorrow."

Ben nodded in affirmation and tucked the brochure into his coat pocket.

A moment later the waitress arrived and set an order of blueberry pancakes before Brian and a chicken BLT bread bowl salad before Kay. Ben withdrew a scrap of paper from his pocket and wrote down his cell phone number. He turned back around to face the couple after the waitress departed. "Here, call me when y'all are fixin' to meet up again."

Brian took the scrap of paper and handed it to Kay. She appeared to examine the paper carefully and then pocketed it.

Ben smiled politely, holding his gaze extra long at Kay. She did not appear to be bothered by this and smiled warmly in return. He turned back around and withdrew his cell phone from his jacket pocket to check for missed calls. One text message just arrived. Again, it was from James Malloy.

We've got problems. What did u use for a device? Investigators tell me they're running tests on some items they found.

Ben entered in a reply. *y u pressing charges?*

I'm not. The landowners are. Whatever you did to the pond spread to the grass. I'm pretty sure I can get them to drop the charges.

A minute went by.

Malloy texted again. *Can I get an answer to what I asked you about before?*

Ben did not reply.

Can I get an answer?

Ben clapped his cell phone shut and tucked the phone back into his coat pocket. He then sprinkled salt and pepper on his Everything Omelet and plunged his fork into its overstuffed contents. As he downed a forkful of green peppers, cheese, tomatoes and egg, he thought how in the end he knew the investigators might eventually hit a dead end anyway.

He heard the man behind him whisper, "What if the guy's a plant?"

The woman replied, "You worry too much, Brian."

Chapter Nineteen

It was seven o'clock in the evening, on a moonless Friday night in the fourth week of October when Alex made a phone call he knew he would later regret. He sat at his desk chair at work and rubbed the beginnings of a beard before picking up the phone. Charles and Drew went home hours ago, which was a wise act, he reasoned, as the three of them argued most of the day anyway.

He dialed home and waited as the phone rang three times. Finally, his wife answered.

"Hi, Danielle?" Alex said.

"Yes?"

"It's Alex I have some bad news."

"Tell me something new for once."

He drew in a deep breath and stared at one of his computer monitors. "The builds are taking longer than I thought. Lots of stupid bugs."

Danielle did not respond.

"So, uh, I'm going to have to take a rain check on our dinner date tonight."

He cringed as those last words came out.

Again, there was more silence. In the background he could hear David asking a question, and for a moment, he could tell she held her hand over the mouthpiece of the phone. It sounded as if he asked something about his clothes.

Alex fidgeted with a pencil on his desk. "Danielle? You still there?"

"Uh huh."

"Something wrong?"

"No. It's fine."

"You're not saying much."

"Just come home whenever."

Alex rubbed his forehead. "I'm trying. I really am."

"Anybody else there with you?"

That's a strange question, he thought to himself.

"No. Just me. Like I said, I'm trying to get out of here. I'll make it up to you this weekend. We'll go to a Chinese place. Just you and I."

"I know."

Then, more silence.

"So how was your day?" He said, unsure of how to direct the conversation. Again, it sounded like she cupped her hand over the mouthpiece of the phone.

"Can I talk to you later? I was in the middle of something when you called."

"Okay. Sure."

He hung up the phone, but something in the tone of her voice made him nervous. There was a cryptic minimalism he could not fathom and a hidden agenda in her conversation with David. He shook off the thought and downed a last gulp of cold coffee which began to taste like an ashtray smelled.

He stood up and left his office to go to the break room. He passed by the office photocopier and chuckled. Earlier in the day, Raj taped an "out of order" sign on top of the machine with a frazzled smiley face on it. He wandered into the break room and poured the last of the coffee out of the decanter. One gaze over at the contents of the vending machine did more to upset his stomach than spark his appetite.

On the way back to his office, he decided to stop by the server room and test bench area. On one of the green-topped test benches stood a computer monitor, a portable oscilloscope, a pair of digital meters, and several palm-sized circuit boards with multiple cables running out of them. Above that was a rack of well-worn manuals and a spaghetti tangle of alligator clip wires and RCA plugs. To the left of that on the floor sat four workstation computers stacked on top of one another, the top one having its outer shell removed. On another bench were several hard drives of various sizes and capacities, with one disassembled and rendered useless.

Shuffling across the concrete floor he peered on at the two rows of server racks which stood like bookcases full of pizza-box sized, black and silver components. He did not fully understand why they would need such a purchase, considering their company website was nothing elaborate, nor did it entertain a heavy traffic load. A sense of unfamiliarity swept over him as the room had been rearranged weeks ago to accommodate the two new racks of servers. The Pegasus project never required such a setup, even in the prisons where it was being tested. Plans remained in the works for something big, he figured, and he peered behind each of the racks to see a waterfall of blue and light gray cables.

Shaking his head, he meandered back to the lonely confines of his office. He passed another table full of Ethernet cables of various lengths by the door and felt an eerie sense of purpose wash over him. Normally, he prided himself on knowing what the hardware side of the company was doing, and he admitted to himself he spent a little too much time in the isolation of his office as of late. Sure, he would have visitors daily. Yet his concentration over both the Möbius and the Pegasus projects wreaked havoc with his sense of time.

Dowsing the lights to the test area, he caught a glimpse of a stack of Pegasus rings next the table of cables. Next to that, were three receiver modules. *Routine*, he thought, except the rings were painted bright blue and noticeably thinner.

Returning to his office, he looked at the calendar. Halloween loomed just days away. Around his neighborhood one found candlelit jack-o'-lanterns, orange pumpkin lawn bags, and an abundance of leaves shuffling about on the ground. He doubted any raking around the yard would ever get done by the time the first snow fell.

At his desk, he took one last look over an error handler function which had become the pride of the last hour for him. He tried to compensate for every single act of garbage input he could think of that could come in through the database's record searching interface. He fired off the integrated development environment's compiler to make the latest build, which had the arduous task of lexing and parsing the code, and then linking it together with other object code and header files to produce the final, polished executable.

As it ran, he put his head onto his desk. He stared at a pair of open programming manuals in front of him and smiled. Then, he closed his eyes for what he hoped was a five minute nap.

* * *

His slumber was interrupted by something that sounded like somebody opening a fiercely shaken can of soda. That was followed by the sound of breaking glass. He opened his eyes to a crackling sound and detected a faint odor of smoke. For a moment, he thought he fell into another dream, but one pinch of his arm told him otherwise. After rubbing his burning eyes, he jumped up out of his chair and called out.

"Hello?"

He rounded his desk, nearly tripping on the carpet, and left his office. Following the odor and the noise, he poked his head into Charles' office. He immediately noticed the carpeting in Charles' office had bloomed into flame. Smoke billowed up towards the ceiling, fanning out along the tiles. The flames ate away at the carpet with alarming speed. Without thinking, he ran towards the break room.

He searched high and low around in the cupboards for a bucket of some sort. Instead he found a dusty, emerald-green, plastic party bowl on top of the refrigerator. A leftover from last Christmas no doubt. He grabbed it, slipped it under the faucet and cranked on the water full blast.

Darting into the server room he found a fire extinguisher. The thing felt like it weighed a good forty pounds fully loaded, but anything at this point would have to do. As he reentered the main reception area, he was confronted by a thickening haze. He choked on the fumes which reeked of burning cables and gasoline.

Unhooking the extinguisher nozzle, he squeezed the trigger and sprayed Charles' office with as much foam as he could. By now the unquenchable flames ignited the ceiling tiles and flames leapt out of the office and into the hallway. He expended as much of the extinguisher as he could but the smoke overpowered his senses and some of the foam blew back into his face.

He ditched the extinguisher and ran back into the break room. The party bowl overflowed with water and he began to hear strange popping noises in the ceiling. As he ran out with the bowl of water the power in the building failed. The flames kindled the tiles in the reception area, causing one tile to drop to the floor. He stomped on the tile in an attempt to put out the flames, and for a second, it caught his brown dress shoe on fire.

He flung off his shoe and splashed some of the water on it. After it hissed and sizzled a moment, he slipped the shoe back on and charged into Charles' office.

Alex threw the bowl full of water into the office, aiming for the worst part of the fire. With a loud hiss, some of the flames were smothered, triggering another cloud of smoke. But soon the carpet ignited again because of the heat.

He dodged yet another falling tile as he ran back into his own office, covering his mouth with his shirt sleeve. In the dark, he found a cardboard box and began throwing his personal belongings inside. He tossed in books, discs, and pages of printed code. The heat from the flames began to raise the temperature of his office, too, and soon he ditched his suit coat by flinging it into the corner.

He threw his briefcase into the box, along with some notes from his boss.

Then some pages of ideas.

And a picture of Danielle and David.

Keys!

He sighed and made a dash for the door. Snapping orange dragons of flame blocked his path and another smoking tile crashed onto his head. He swung wildly and brushed the embers out of his hair.

In the smothering blackness, he felt for his desk chair. Seizing it with both hands, he rolled it around the edge of his desk and hurled it at what he thought was his office window. The chair slammed into the wall, knocking some pictures to the floor in a crash of metal and breaking glass. He clutched the box under one arm and felt his way towards where the window should have been and held his breath.

He found the window latch, but it was now hot to the touch. Desperate for a way out, he felt around for his suit coat since he threw it over here moments earlier. By now his office was completely full of toxic smoke. He coughed hard as he found his suit coat on the floor.

With great effort, he wrapped the coat around his hand. Sweat poured off his forehead and into his eyes, mixing with the smoke particles in the air. With a violent jerk, he sprung the window latch open and forced the window up with his arm. With his shoe he kicked out the screen and threw the box out after it. He then climbed through the window, gasping for air as he tumbled to the ground.

Tongues of flame shot out from his window behind him and from Charles's office. By now smoke was already pouring into the sky. He dug into his pants pocket for his cell phone. As he powered it on, he coughed up something that tasted like copper. Hands shaking, he dialed 911.

Chapter Twenty

Alex sat dazed on the lawn, and waited for the fire department to arrive. From the building he heard more popping noises as the flames ignited something on the roof. Fortunately, there was little wind tonight, although there was plenty of fuel for the blaze with all the books and boxes of papers scattered throughout their offices. He dialed his boss on his phone, but Drew's answering machine answered instead.

"Hi, Drew? It's Alex from work. It's about seven-thirty and the company's on fire. I'm okay."

He hung up and heard glass breaking around the back side of the building. He stood up and walked around the perimeter of the building near his office and near Charles' office. Dried, fallen leaves swished and crunched underfoot, and the thought crossed his mind that the entire area could potentially be a fuel source.

Through the heat, smoke, and flames he could see what appeared to be a hole in Charles' window, perhaps where something had been thrown. That window promptly popped out, spewing sparks and glass, sending Alex scampering backwards.

He scanned the parking lot and the nearby woods for signs of activity. He sprinted up to the edge of the trees and scanned the ground for something—anything—that might lend a clue. For what it was worth, he shouted a couple of times, but heard no reply. He walked back to his box of belongings and carried them over to the trunk of his car.

In less than five minutes a fire truck and two police cars arrived in a chorus of sirens and flashing lights. Several firefighters jumped out of the truck, and one of them shone a spotlight in the direction of a nearby fire hydrant. Two men quickly uncoiled a hose and lugged it towards the hydrant. Another firefighter jumped out of the truck and approached Alex.

"What happened?" The firefighter asked.

"I don't know," Alex said. "I heard a fizzing noise or something like that and then a popping sound. Then there was a crash and the next thing I know there's fire everywhere."

"You injured or anything?"

Alex briefly explained his escape but waved off the suggesting of seeing a medic.

"Alright. Anything dangerous inside we should know about? Chemicals? Fuel? That sorta stuff?"

"Nah. Wait. Lots of books and papers. Maybe a few cans of paint in the test lab."

"Do you know if anybody else is in the building?"

"No. Just me, I think."

The firefighter nodded and then turned around to talk with another colleague. Alex looked back to see the men attaching the hose to the hydrant. In another part of the parking lot, two police officers stepped out of their squad cars. It was a cacophony of sound with the roar of the burning building, the humming of the fire truck, and the crackling sounds of the police radios nearby.

Five minutes later, Drew pulled up in his white Lexus and parked next to Alex's car. By the time Drew stepped out of his car, the firefighters just started to pump dozens of gallons of water onto the remnants of his business. Drew began to walk entranced towards Alex, apparently forgetting to shut his own car door.

"Are you okay?" He said.

"I'm fine," Alex shouted back.

"What happened?"

Alex recounted the night from the perspective of his desk. "Everything I could salvage is here in this box. Unfortunately, it's mostly my stuff."

He wanted to press Drew about insurance, and whether the company had any for the building or anything inside, but watched as Drew appeared to be in shock. No words of comfort surged to mind, and all he desired to do now was to leave.

Drew turned back towards Alex. "Did you give a statement to the police?"

"Not yet."

He knew his clothing reeked of burnt plastic and smoke, and the odor made him nauseous. He slammed his trunk shut and stood next to Drew. "I'd stick around, but my clothes stink and I'm cold. After this I'm going home. It's best that I leave anyway."

"What makes you say that?"

"Trust me. I have to go. This is probably my fault."

Drew reached out a hand and grabbed the edge of Alex's dirtied shirt. "How is this *your fault?* I don't understand. Did something catch fire in the break room?"

"No, no. Drew, I think somebody was aiming for me."

"Who? Did you tell the police? Here, come over there with me. If this was arson, I'm pressing charges right now."

"I'll tell them." Alex paced towards a nearby squad car, but stopped for a minute because of a sneezing fit.

Drew put an arm on Alex's shoulder from behind. "Do you need an escort? Is someone after you? I want to know."

"No, no escort."

For the first time since Alex could remember, Drew stood speechless. He then walked over to an officer to give her a statement. As he relayed his account, he saw Drew's silhouette against the backdrop of the remaining flames, head hung low. Tonight his boss was wearing a black tee-shirt, jeans, and of course, his favorite sneakers. Out of the corner of his eye, Alex could even see some of the flames reflecting off of his glasses. *How do you counsel a man on something like this?*

After giving the officer his statement, he climbed into his car and pulled away. His heart drummed away inside his chest, in sudden concern about his family. Would the arsonist, whoever it was, be so low as to aim for them?

* * *

As Alex pulled into his garage, he noticed Danielle's car was missing. It was eight-thirty in the evening, so although her absence was a bit unusual, it was not unprecedented. He rolled up his driver side window since he drove home with the windows down and the heater on full blast. It was obvious he was going to have to shampoo the interior of the car just to get the smoke odor out.

Shaking, he slid out of the car, and opened the trunk. He pulled out the smoke-tainted cardboard box that represented the pieces of his personal life at work. With a sigh, he slammed the trunk shut and entered the house.

On the basement level, he noticed no lights were on. As he hiked up the stairs from the lower level, he found himself in a scene filled with silence. No dishwasher sounds, no television chatter, no radio noise. No lights were on except a light over the stove.

He set his box down on the dining room table. On one end of the table, he spotted the Bible laying open to Psalm 130. With a slam, he flipped the cover shut. He turned on the dining room light, then the main kitchen light, and plodded into his bedroom.

He flipped on yet another light and froze upon peering into the closet.

A suitcase was missing.

He lurched back into the hallway and bolted into the living room. The television, still there, along with the DVD player, sat immense and silent. Nothing appeared to be missing in the kitchen. He charged into the bathroom, yet nothing appeared disturbed. With a swift lunge, he peered into David's room. A few dresser drawers were half open, and he could see a few shirts, socks, and pairs of underwear were missing. His bed remained unmade from the morning.

He flew downstairs, skipping several risers in the process and flung the garage service door open with a bang. An automatic light came on. He scanned the walls of the garage. None of his tools appeared to be missing on his workbench in the corner. The lawnmower was still there. Rakes, a shovel, the garden hoe, and the garden hose all remained undisturbed and hanging on the walls around the garage.

* * *

James Malloy stepped out of his car in the Woodbury 10 Theater parking lot and approached the lobby with Susan at his side. The front of the theater was made of tan brick, with six, tiered, illuminated columns rising high above the lobby doors. The columns appeared to be made of glass block windows and were trimmed with red, blue and green lighting. The columns were joined at the front by a rectangular, vertical sign that read "Woodbury".

James eyed the horizontal marquees on either side of the vertical sign, but none of the titles seemed attractive tonight. Together, they entered the lobby doors and waited in a line that nearly snaked outside the door. Malloy pulled out his PDA and began to poke at it with a stylus.

He noted that a new e-mail message just arrived from Ben. With a poke of the stylus, he opened it. "What the…"

"What is it?" Susan said.

The answer is behind you.

Malloy quickly moved to the next message in his inbox before Susan could see it and pretended to look at some grade school kids running around in the lobby. He then glanced over at the concession counter, but noticed nothing unusual. As not to draw too much attention to himself, he turned around casually and tried to see into the parking lot. He squinted as he caught sight of an orange glow in the distance. If he had his bearings right that would be just about the location of…

"Hoyle," he said under his breath.

"What?" Susan said.

"Grab our tickets. I'm going to make a call real quick."

"But what movie? James. Honestly. Give me that…"

Before she could grab his PDA he pushed through the crowd and out the door. As he stood outside he pretended to dial his phone. In truth, he wanted to get a better view of the orange glow from the parking lot. The sight of smoke confirmed his worst fears. He could smell the odor of smoke now on the wind. He swore to himself and swooped back inside, dropping enough f-bombs on the way to destroy multiple conversations. He elbowed his way back to Susan, who was now within a few minutes of the ticket counter.

Malloy stared at the indoor marquee a moment. It was a slow time of year for movies, that was for sure.

"What was that all about?" Susan said, with a cynical look in her eyes. "Honestly, can you break free from that fool thing for two hours?"

Malloy kept his voice low. "The building's afire."

"Here?!"

"No, no. Keep your voice down." He leaned over to whisper in her ear. "Hoyle-Aspen."

"I don't follow."

Malloy shook his head and rolled his eyes. "They're making rings for us."

"Oh."

"Some punk just sent me a message saying 'here's your answer'. If you turn around real slow, you might be able to see it in the distance."

She spun around and jumped up in the air to try and see into the parking lot. Several members of the crowd began to turn around, too, and some even began to point fingers in the general direction of the fire.

Malloy cringed and whispered to her. "Stop staring, you're making a scene!" He continued to poke at his PDA and retrieved the e-mail from Ben again. He noticed it was from an unfamiliar e-mail address, however, and one with the word 'lamps' in it. He let a broad smile explode across his face.

"Rookie mistake," he said to himself in a low rumbling voice. He racked his brain trying to think of where he had heard of 'lamps' before.

Oh yes, he thought. Now he remembered their literature arriving many, many months ago in his inbox.

"Are you okay?" Susan said, glaring at him.

"No. I mean, yes."

Susan crossed her arms and inched forward in line.

Malloy put his hands in his pockets and frowned. His stomach began to tighten up and he felt beads of sweat forming on his forehead.

"Should we leave?" She said.

"No. It's just...it's them."

"Them? Who? You sound paranoid."

"Shh. Not so loud." He put his PDA away. "Seems the little punk wants to make a name for himself. He's joined up with some troublemakers. But they've been on my radar a long time. So help me tomorrow I'm going to have reports pulled on all of them. I'll tag 'em like cattle."

Susan gave him a confused look, contorting her lips into an 'S' shaped curve.

Malloy became agitated and expressive with his hand gestures. "There's a group I've been keeping tabs on. They've got plans to shut us down, Sue."

Her eyes bugged out a moment, but before she could speak again, he cut her off. "My Dad, he used to have these friends over. Biggest bunch of hypocrites you ever seen. Oh but were they ever holy on Sunday, I tell you. Then he'd take off with 'em and their traveling circus tent revivals or whatever they were."

She rolled her eyes and crept forward in line. They were now two people away from the counter.

"For the last time, Jim, who is *them*? What are you talking about?"

"The Jesus kooks."

Chapter Twenty-One

Alex bolted back into the house and ran back into the kitchen. His heart knocked inside of his ribcage like a failing piston. Out of breath, he searched across the counter and then spied a note being held up by a magnet on the refrigerator. It was in Danielle's handwriting. He snatched the cordless phone off of its charger and pulled the note off of the door.

According to the note, she left with David and went to her parents' house in Corcoran for the weekend. She was taking time out to help her mother out around the house and would return in a couple of days. He dialed her mother's telephone number, yet there was no answer.

He returned to the dining room and sunk into a chair. He set the phone down and slipped off his socks and shirt. He stared on at the lone box he brought home from his workplace. Where would the next mortgage payment come from? What would cover the car payment on the vehicle he was driving? Sure, they had savings, but only a few months worth.

His breathing intensified until he took one deep, loud breath in an effort to settle his nerves. He felt like walking, no, *running*, around the perimeter of the house to make sure the plans of the arsonist were not bigger.

Tilting the box from his office towards him, he sifted through its contents. Beneath the family photos, the watercolor art, the drawings and the books lay a diagram and pages of printed code. He pulled them out and set the stack on the table. Among the code samples was a photograph of the planned retail version ring.

Shuddering, he stuffed the code under his arm. He went over towards the refrigerator and rooted through the cupboards for matches. Upon finding a tattered, half-spent matchbook, he seized it and held it up to the ceiling light. Alex knew he was the only engineer who could fix the database systems now, and carry them into the future that Charles envisioned. As such, Alex was the keeper of the code and its documentation, and knew it was his responsibility to discern the way forward.

The way forward, Alex thought, *was to finish off what was left in his possession*. The code seemed to radiate heat of its own under his arm now, and he almost felt that his own body heat would help ignite it to flame. He panned around the room. There were two smoke alarms in the house that would surely go off with the cloud of smoke a two-inch thick stack of burning paper would create.

He scrambled downstairs, walked through the game room, and opened the sliding glass doors to the concrete patio outside. He eyed the barbecue grill. With one hand, he twisted off the black, shiny domed top. He pulled out the circular grilling rack and laid the code to rest on top of some charcoal cinders in the bottom of the bowl.

Without thinking further, he struck a match. Then another. Then another and another until all the corners of the printouts ignited. The flames soon converged into one large orange plume. As the flames licked the ink off of the printouts, he watched it like the burning of a book or a painting melting into oblivion.

Sure, his skills would always stay with him, he reasoned. There was a certain art to coding—behind the befuddling marriage of cryptic phrases, numbers, and logic which often greeted the untrained eye. He knew in his heart there were often an endless amount of answers to a given problem, but company time, limited resources, efficiency, security, and maintainability often put constraints in place. Yet every new creation, every problem solved was an achievement to behold, he thought, and his creations always returned a sense of fondness to the him as time passed.

As the flames burned themselves out Alex looked up to feel a gentle rain falling on his face and shoulders. The concrete deck was damp and cold beneath his feet. He could see his breath now, too. A cool breeze came in, and he twisted the grill lid back into place, ensuring the vents on top were closed.

Barefoot and broken, he stepped back inside and lumbered up the stairs. Once he reached the living room, however, the energy drained out of him like someone pulling the plug in a sink full of water. He walked over to the couch and collapsed a minute later.

* * *

Todd Oliver opened his apartment door, tired from a day of running his own computer repair shop, TKO Computer Repair. He tossed his car keys onto the kitchen counter and flipped on the kitchen light. The apartment was quiet, almost too quiet, and his cat Charcoal did not come up to meet him as usual.

He leaned over to look alongside the counter to check on her water and food bowls. Nothing appeared abnormal. On the kitchen table, he found his television's remote control, which was an odd place for him to leave it. He aimed it at the television in hopes he was in time to watch some championship boxing on ESPN.

He called out Charcoal's name. He checked on the couch, under the couch, and behind the couch. There was no sign of her on or behind his brown recliner, either. He returned to the kitchen and checked in the cupboards and called out her name again.

Upon hearing no reply, he wandered over to his bedroom door. He noticed his door was shut tight as usual. His brother Sean's door, however, was open a crack.

"Charcoal?"

Inside his brother's bedroom he heard stirring and what sounded like a tiny meow. Although he never entered his brother's room without permission, tonight would be an exception, or so he told himself. He pushed on the open door and was startled to see an obnoxious mess of a room. Clothes, magazines and papers were laying all over the floor. The bed was unmade. A half-eaten bowl of chocolate chip ice cream sat on the dresser, melted from the day before.

"Charcoal?"

Again he heard a tiny meow. He got down and peered underneath Sean's bed and in addition to the usual sets of tennis shoes were more clothes and some crumpled newspapers. Behind him he heard papers shuffling. He looked back towards the closet. There, in the corner he could see two green glowing eyes staring back at him.

He got up and snuck over to the closet to find her looking up from a cardboard box. He reached in to pull her out and accidentally grabbed a handful of papers along with her. Charcoal, the brown and black striped alley cat, purred in his arms as if she'd done nothing wrong.

"There you are, my little green eyed lady."

Todd carried her back out and into the hallway and went back inside the bedroom, closing the door behind him. He picked up the papers off the floor and examined them before setting them back inside the cardboard box in the closet. On the two sheets he picked up, he found what appeared to be names, bank account numbers, routing numbers, and several attempts at fake signatures.

He marched back over to the closet and pulled out the box. Buried under some newspapers were more papers covered in account numbers, blank payroll checks, a couple of USB flash drives, and at the bottom of the box, a black Toshiba Satellite notebook computer. In disgust, he shoved the box back into the closet, not caring if it looked like that when he initially found it.

He charged back into the living room, still carrying the two papers with the account numbers and slammed the bedroom door closed. Charcoal, who was waiting at the door, sprung backwards and scampered off into the kitchen.

Todd stopped to look over the names and numbers again, stroking his black mustache and beard. He craved a smoke, and bad. One name on the list jumped out at him: Alex Poole, an ex co-worker. Sure enough, his home address matched, too. He sighed loud and tucked the papers into his jeans pocket. Sean would come home any minute and at the least, this would be a confrontation to remember.

He returned to the kitchen and found his cigarettes. With several sharp cracks, he packed his cigarettes and then set the box back onto the counter. As he withdrew a cigarette, he shook his head and then grabbed his emerald-green disposable lighter. With a couple quick flicks, he lit up a smoke and crossed through the living room and over to the deck. He opened the deck door to a cool, October evening breeze. In reality, though, he wanted to go a few rounds in the boxing ring down at the gym, or better yet, beat the tar out of a punching bag.

Moments later, he heard the lock on his apartment door turn. He took a final pull off of his cigarette, grimaced, and then snuffed out the butt on the rusty deck railing. Returning inside, he slid the glass deck doors closed and stared on at his brother, Sean. His brother entered the living room and sat on the couch, looking at something on his cell phone.

Sean looked up. "What?"

Todd continued to stare and watched as Sean put his feet up on the couch. When standing, he was about five-foot-four. His brother had a brutally short haircut, a narrow, long nose and a gaunt look to his face. The man looked as if he had not slept in a few days.

Todd sat down on a recliner adjacent to the couch. A smirk crossed his face, but soon departed. "How's the new job going?" He began coolly.

"Fine. Lots of work tonight."

"Really? When's payday?"

"Next Friday."

Todd turned his attention to the boxing match on the television and chuckled to himself. "You never change do you?"

Sean turned to face his brother. "Don't worry. You'll get the rent money."

"If you're going to pay it with a rubber check, you can keep it."

Sean rolled his eyes. "When have I ever paid you with a bad check?"

"Never. You pay in cash. Cash from a bad check, maybe?"

"When have I ever passed a bum check?"

Todd pointed a finger at Sean. "Listen, don't go this road with me. I took you in for a reason. I always said you could talk to me. So when I find things like this…"

Todd reached into his pocket. He pulled the papers out and held them up in the air. "I get a little suspicious."

"What's that?"

"I found them earlier today. Where'd you get these?"

"What is it?"

"Names. Addresses. Account numbers."

"It's not mine."

Todd leaned forward and flashed the papers at him. "I said, where'd *you* get these?"

"Get a clue. *Not mine.*"

Sean leapt up off the couch and went into his bedroom, still pushing the buttons on his cell phone. A moment later he shouted. "Hey! Why were you in my room?"

"I want to know who gave you this crap. There's a guy on here that I used to work with. So you can make this easy or really hard on yourself. Pick carefully."

Todd jumped up and walked over to Sean's bedroom door. He swooped in to push Sean against the wall by the collar of his shirt.

Sean swore. "What's your problem, man?"

"You doing this junk in my place is the problem. Lemme ask you again in case you got a short memory, *man*." Todd stressed the word man in a sarcastic tone of voice.

"Put me down."

Todd continued to press Sean against the wall with enough force to make him cough.

"I found them at a bar, okay?"

"Bull. You stole them."

"I didn't steal them. I told you I found them. On a table."

"Who would leave this around in a bar? Seriously? Think for a minute."

When no answer came, Todd lifted him up off the carpet by his shoulders.

Sean swore. "Your breath stinks."

"Tell me you didn't write a bunch of bad checks with this. Tell me you didn't go around town cashing them."

Sean attempted to kick Todd in the kneecap, but Todd backed away and dropped his brother to the floor like a sack of cat litter. Sean fell into a heap but pushed himself back up onto his feet. He bolted to his dresser and crammed several pairs of underwear and a sweatshirt into a black backpack.

Todd pulled a hand through his own hair in frustration. "Where you think you're going?"

"Out."

Sean threw his backpack over his shoulder and snapped up a sleeping bag out of the closet. Shaking and pale, he shoved his way past Todd and out of the room. In a second, he dove for the front door, and sprinted out into the hallway.

Todd slammed the bedroom door shut and ran after Sean, but stopped in the hall in front of his apartment door. He slammed his fist on the wall and stomped back into the apartment. With a slam of the door, he headed back towards Sean's bedroom to take a closer look at the laptop. A picture of a sailboat in the Pacific Ocean came crashing down off the living room wall with a bang.

On his way past the kitchen he eyed his pack of cigarettes again. Quitting that habit would have to wait for another night.

Chapter Twenty-Two

The following day Alex awoke a few minutes after noon to stark silence. The odor of stale, sickly smoke hung in the air. He felt exhausted, as if he had just ran a marathon, yet his mind kept trying to keep him awake. He lay there on the couch studying the cold, glass-shuttered fireplace before him. On top of the mantel were several miniature, deep orange pumpkins, lined up in a row. Danielle's words came flooding back to him.

At least I can make veggies grow.

A tear welled up in his eye. His eyes then drifted down to see some of David's toys sitting on the floor. David had left a red and white plastic fire engine and a hand-sized, plastic F-16 fighter jet lying in between the coffee table and the television set. To the right of that was his favorite stuffed animal—a black and white panda bear named Pepper.

He sat up and felt stiffness in his neck. On the top of his head he discovered a scab of some sort. Near that he found a small patch of dried blood, possibly from the falling tiles or the escape through the window. His pants were covered in soot and dirt, with a burn hole near his ankle. At some point he knew would have to have the couch carpet-cleaned after this.

Against the wishes of his body, he forced himself up off the couch. His legs felt heavy as he moved about the house. Worse yet, the overwhelming silence bothered him. From the coffee table he grabbed the remote control and fired a single shot at the television, bringing it to life.

He then trudged into the kitchen and poured himself a heaping bowl of Marshmallow Mateys. With patient steps, he carried the bowl over to the dining room table and sat down. The television chattered away incessantly, and the noise was better than the silence, even if it was somewhat artificial. He changed the channels several times, but little held his interest for more than a half minute.

On his left sat the Bible from the bookcase, which he closed last night of course. Inside his heart, however, he sensed something different today.

A phrase suddenly came into his mind: *Open the Word.*

He ignored the moment and finished his cereal. He returned to the kitchen, rinsed his bowl and noticed for the first time that there were several dirty dishes stacked up in the sink from the day before. Although it would have been easy to load the plates, bowls and a pan of caked macaroni-and-cheese into the dishwasher, he felt no energy to do so. Instead, like a scene out of an abandoned restaurant, he set the bowl on top of the stack and headed for his bedroom.

When he flicked on the bedroom light, he was struck again by the neatness of the bed which remained untouched from the morning before. He noticed a few of Danielle's clothes missing from the closet, and again a tear welled up in his eye. Part of him wanted to run to the telephone and call her immediately. Instead, he forced himself to find a set of clothes and go take a shower.

* * *

In the afternoon Alex visited Abernathy's grocery store. The usual Saturday crowd kept most of the fifteen registers hopping, with a steady flow of customers in and out of the store. The time in public allowed him some sense of belonging, if only in terms of his purpose there, but at the same time let him think through the events of last night alone. For some reason, he could not get the initial sound he heard at his desk out of his head. It reminded him so much of an exploding can of soda, or maybe more like the sound of a large firework being set off in the driveway. Almost as if something flew at the window in Charles' office...

After loading his cart full of groceries, he stood in line and watched a teenage, strawberry-blonde, female clerk finish up with the customer in front of him. She wore a pale red shirt and black pants, but she seemed impatient at best, as if she already had finished her shift in her mind.

He studied the customer in front of him as they handed over a pale blue check. The customer was an Indian woman in her mid-twenties, with dark, coiled-up hair, and wearing a highly colorful sari. Her two year old son kicked away happily in the shopping cart. The clerk examined the check quickly, and passed it through a check-verification machine. The check was then slipped into the till and the drawer closed.

The black conveyor belt jerked to life again. As each item passed over the scanner, Alex thought about how it was registering upstairs on the store office monitors. He wheeled his cart to the end of the aisle and popped open a pair of paper bags in earnest. Canned vegetables, a bag of celery, a head of lettuce, and a carton of eggs soon moved down the belt towards him. The second-to-last item to be scanned was a cardboard box full of canned, condensed soup.

"Are these all the same kind?" The clerk asked.

"No," Alex said. "The cans are all different. All twenty of them."

With a noticeable frown, she pulled each can of soup across the scanner. By the twentieth can, he watched her practically toss the whole box onto his side of the conveyor belt. He glanced up towards the offices he visited weeks earlier and hoped somebody was watching. Was that a bit spiteful? He was in no shape to judge that. The last item she dragged across the scanner was a bag of potato chips which she threw to the side.

When she finished, she read the total off of the register screen. Alex withdrew his Aspirizon Bank card and slid it through the card reader in the middle of the lane. His shoulders tensed up a moment, as he somehow figured it would be a repeat of what happened to him weeks ago in the gas station. Fortunately, the card reader beeped and the cash register drawer popped open. The clerk shoved the drawer shut with her knee.

"By the way. I have a question," said Alex. "Why didn't you ask for an i.d. from the last woman in line? She wrote a check."

"I've seen her in here before."

"How about me? Have you seen me before?"

"Sure," she said half-heartedly, popping a bubble with her gum.

Alex signed his name on the display in front of him with a tethered, plastic stylus. She snapped the receipt off of the register, handed it over to Alex, and then began to scan the next customers' groceries. He walked down to the end of the checkout lane and set the celery and the lettuce into one of the bags.

"Then why was someone else able to walk in here a few weeks ago, claim they were me and able to pass a check in my name?" He said suddenly.

The clerk stopped a moment then started to fight with the UPC code on a bag of cereal. The scanner refused to cooperate and so she jabbed in the product number on her register keypad. With a slap, she flung the bag of cereal onto the conveyer belt opposite Alex.

"Ma'am, you might want to take your time and check identification next time," Alex said after a minute.

She stopped for a moment, put a hand on her hip, and glared at Alex. "I'm sorry to hear that, sir. I'll make sure it gets enforced."

In response, the clerk moved each item faster over the scanner now. The Indian woman next to Alex finished bagging the last of her fresh vegetables but looked on in horror as a wave of groceries came down the belt at her at record speed. With a crunch, the first items were smashed up against the end of the lane. Another customer in line turned and whispered something to her husband.

"I hope you do enforce it," Alex said as he stacked some microwave dinners into a grocery bag. "Because you may be the last line of defense someone like me has. In more ways than you know."

Alex left the store and put the groceries into the trunk of his car. After that, he pushed the cart into a corral and walked into Abernathy's liquor store next door. It had been a while since he visited there, but he immediately locked in on the beer section as soon as he walked in the door.

He ignored the wine racks and the colorful assortment of hard liquors, and instead grabbed himself a six pack out of the cooler. With a clunk, he dropped it onto the counter. Again, without thinking, he pulled out his Aspirizon Bank card and gave it to the cashier. After a driver's license check and a swipe of the card, he was gone.

* * *

Back home, Alex unloaded the groceries on the kitchen counter. He set the six pack of beer into the refrigerator and tore off a can. He held it in his hand a moment, read the label, and let its coldness soak into his hand. Then he set it back on the shelf. Somehow the thought of getting blasted on the couch with some old movies did not seem so interesting anymore.

He finished up unloading the grocery bags and noticed out of the corner of his eye that the answering machine light was blinking. He hit the playback button on the machine.

"Hi, Alex. It's Drew. Uh, just checking on how you're doing. Give me a call."

The machine beeped and said "end of messages" in a male, mechanical voice. He erased the message and picked up the phone. Again, he dialed Drew's number, but the phone rang four times without an answer. He reached an answering machine and left a message.

He felt an urge to call his wife again, but suppressed it. Then he thought about calling his parents, but instead figured there was a good chance this whole blowup with Danielle would blow over in a weekend anyway. Why stress them out, too?

He wandered over to the card table in the corner of the kitchen with the puzzle still sprawled out on top of it. A pile of pieces still sat near the outer edge of the picture, separated neatly into colored piles. At once, he began to plug in the black, white and gray pieces near the bottom of the puzzle, where a series of jagged ocean rocks should be, at least according to the picture on the box.

Again, a phrase came into his mind: *Open the Word.*

Looking up, he turned back towards the dining room table and stared again at the closed Bible. With a snap, he plugged in another piece of rock and walked over to the other table and sat down.

Often, as a boy, he felt the urge to read it cover to cover, but for many years he ignored it. He recalled now how he once flipped open his parents' Bible on the kitchen table one rainy afternoon and how he made a pledge to himself to copy it by hand, cover to cover, book by book. Logically, it made no sense, but he began scribbling the first three chapters of Genesis onto loose-leaf notebook paper. He became familiar with all the names of the books of the Bible, but gave up his copying ambitions after he started chapter four.

Outside, the clouds played with the sunlight coming in through the curtains of the room, changing the lighting abruptly at times. Maybe, like that afternoon as a child, he thought, the sun would give way to rain, too, keeping him inside for a while.

He flipped the Bible open at random and found he opened it up to the Book of Jonah. Within twenty minutes, he read that particular book all the way through for the fun of it.

Twice.

Chapter Twenty-Three

The handle of the church door was cold and clammy to the touch. Through the glass of the door, Alex could see several adults roaming about and several children running to and fro in the hallway. He pulled on the handle, hoping he picked the least conspicuous entrance to the church this Sunday morning, and slipped inside.

On his left were coat racks where several people were in the process of hanging their jackets. He decided to hang onto his own coat as to avoid any uncomfortable confrontations or explanations when it came time to leave. He reflected on the fact that his family had been to this church years ago, but doubted anybody would recognize him. At best, this thought was a lonely comfort now.

As he progressed through the hallway, he tried to dodge the people scattered through the hallway as if they were rocks in an asteroid field. A short, white-haired man in his seventies with a green nametag that read "Usher" reached out and shook his hand.

"Morning," the man with the nametag said with a warm smile and a strong handshake.

"Morning."

Alex continued on towards the sanctuary, after passing by a table full of brochures, books and signup sheets on his left. To his right was an entrance to a fellowship hall and to the left of that, a set of bathrooms. Here, he found his progress slowed up by a short line of people passing through the wooden double doors of the sanctuary. A family of four handed out pale yellow bulletins to those walking inside.

He felt his heart rate climb a bit and kept his eyes darting around. It was the first time in years he visited a church alone. Part of him wanted to turn around and race for the exit, and he now found himself concocting a list of excuses in case he did leave. Instead, he took a bulletin from a teenage boy and entered the sanctuary.

Once inside, he slipped into an empty pew, furthest in the back, furthest away from the choir chairs and the pipe organ. In silence, he leafed through the bulletin, and scanned it for the order of the service.

Behind him was the gray, concrete block back wall of the sanctuary, and in front, several families. A young boy two pews ahead briefly turned around and smiled at Alex, which only made him think of David. Alex smiled back, then pulled out a pine green hymnal in an attempt to keep himself composed. As he opened the cover, he thought to himself how thankful he should be that he survived the other night. Going a step further and praising God, however, was the last thing he wanted to do right now, though.

He looked on at the large wooden cross on the wall in the front of the sanctuary and reflected on all that it stood for. He then set the hymnal down next to him and withdrew a red-covered Bible from the rack in front of him. Recalling the chapters he read last night, he opened it to the Prayer of Jonah, letting the ending words hit him full force: *"What I have vowed I will make good. Salvation comes from the Lord."*

More families flowed into the sanctuary, filling in the open spaces like a river bursting through a dam. Alex fidgeted with the Bible and felt his body temperature rising. The families all seemed so "connected" with each other, with children holding their mother's hands and some being carried by their fathers. Nobody seemed to be attending alone. Further connections appeared as families and friends passed one another on the way in, shaking hands and chatting with each other.

He set the Bible back into the rack in front of him and then continued to turn the pages of the hymnal, and for a moment, the lighting in the church caught his wedding band at just the right angles. His vision blurred briefly as he stared hard at the only ring that seemed to matter to him anymore.

As the opening hymn began, the congregation stood up. A lone man slipped into his pew, at the far end near the aisle, and then moved closer to Alex as a family of six entered noisily two minutes later. The man slid a slate-colored notepad out of his inside jacket pocket after the hymn ended and began to scribble something with a stubby yellow pencil. He then put the notebook back into his pocket and removed his jacket. He stood several inches shorter than Alex, with thinning brown hair and thin, small-oval glasses.

After the hymn ended, the congregation sat down. Alex leaned over towards the man and quietly said, "Taking notes?"

"Me? Maybe. Sometimes when an idea strikes me I write it down," the man said in a deep baritone voice. "Or during the sermon."

"So, you're a writer?"

"'Fraid not. I'm a copier repairman."

Minutes and verses passed before the congregation seated itself to listen to a series of brief announcements. Alex felt a sudden peace wash over him, undeserved and unexpected. He still could not envision what a cashless collection plate would look like, however.

* * *

At the conclusion of the service, the pews emptied slowly, like receding floodwaters. Alex waited for the copier repairman to stand up. The man wrote something else in his notebook, and, as before, the notebook got tucked away after the thought was finished.

As soon as the man stood up, Alex did, too. When they finally left the pew, they were funneled like everybody else out the back of the sanctuary, and right towards the pastor. He sighed quietly and forced himself to make the best of it. The copier repairman went before him, of course, shook hands with the pastor, and chatted a moment. Then came Alex's turn.

"Great sermon," Alex said, while shaking the man's hand. He hoped the comment would be enough because in truth, his mind was elsewhere for most of the service.

"Thanks. You're…Alex…right?"

"Yeah. That's right. How'd you remember that?"

"I have a long memory. Good to see you again."

Alex was struck by the welcoming sense of peace in the man's voice and by the pastor's incredible memory. The pastor had not changed much over the years, and was a man in his early thirties, with wavy black hair, glasses, and a tinge of a Scottish accent. He smiled broadly at Alex.

Alex then moved out towards the exit door, but the copier repairman inadvertently blocked the way while bending to tie his shoe. At first Alex tried to go around him, but realized there was no room.

The man looked up to notice Alex standing near him. He stood up. "Sorry 'bout that. Say, I hope you don't mind me saying this, but you look like you've had a long night. Any chance there might be something I could pray with you about?"

"No, I'm fine. Thanks anyway. I, uh, have to run, I have somewhere to be right now."

"You sure? You look like you're carrying a burden."

"I'm fine. Really."

The man nodded and let Alex pass on by. Alex slipped through the rest of the crowd towards the exit door. He sensed something distinctly different about this particular little church, although at the moment he could not seem to express it in words. For whatever reason, it took his mind off of a few things, if even for just a few minutes.

* * *

That evening, Alex worked inside of his car to remove the stains and odor from the fire. The inside of his two-car garage was well lit, although it was typically cold this time of year since it was unheated and only insulated on two sides.

He wheeled out his red-and-gray canister-style carpet cleaner onto the garage floor and set it next to the driver's side of his car. He then tore off the black, plastic garbage bags that covered his car seats. It was a quick fix that drew a stare or two from some customers in the grocery store parking lot. He could only imagine what the people at church thought.

After uncoiling the power cord, he plugged the machine in and flipped the power switch. He ran the carpet cleaner's tool over the driver's seat, and then turned to the passenger seat. Halfway through the process, he heard what sounded like a car door slamming shut in his own driveway. With the flick of a switch, he powered down the machine and waited a moment in silence.

Around the side of the house he heard footsteps that reminded him of someone wearing cowboy boots. He backed out of the car and listened. A second later he heard the boots brush some of the bushes out front and climb the front stairs. Then he heard the distinct five-note melody of the doorbell.

He walked over to his workbench and searched for a heavy duty tool of some sort. He picked up a hacksaw, a hammer, and a crowbar in turn. In his mind, he felt none of these tools seemed apt for whoever he might deal with outside his door. As he began to head back inside the house, out of the corner of his eye he noticed an x-wrench.

He picked up the wrench, and clutching it tight with his right hand, entered the house and hiked up the stairs to the front door. The icy, rusty wrench throbbed in his hand, and he cocked his arm back to prepare himself. He then turned on the front light and peered through the security eyelet.

It was Todd Oliver.

Alex opened the door and let his arm drop with the wrench still in it. "Hey. How are you? What are you doing here?"

Todd stood there quietly on the steps, wearing a black leather jacket, a black cowboy hat, blue jeans and cowboy boots. His hands were in his jacket pockets. "Do you have a minute?" He said, in a low rumbling voice.

"Sure, c'mon in." Alex said as he directed Todd to the couch. Todd glanced around the house. "You okay? You look worried."

"You look worried yerself with that wrench in your hand," Todd replied.

Alex gazed down at the wrench and set it onto the recliner. "It's been a long weekend."

"I'll bet. I won't waste your time. But, um, I had a fight last night with Sean."

"Your brother?"

"Right. I don't know if you two ever met. I took him in to live with me after I left Hoyle-Aspen. Kid's got a drug problem. Anyway, I found some papers and a laptop in his room. I was chasing after my cat. I found some of your information, too."

Alex crossed his arms and stood in silence.

"Man, I wanted to box his ears in after I found that out. Claims he found the papers in a bar. I don't buy that, by the way. Later on, I dug out the laptop and found it was *loaded* with bank numbers," Todd said.

Alex narrowed his eyes and walked over to the dining room table.

He picked up his own laptop and carried it into the living room. "Did it look like this?"

Todd leaned forward. "Yeah. Yeah, it did."

"This is getting weird. I saw one of these in a gas station a couple of months ago. No one claimed it when I was there. A friend of mine says they were being found all over the place. All pre-loaded with account data."

Todd swore. "Look man, I'm sorry. Did he do any damage?"

"Some. But my credit's fixed."

Todd shook his head and punched a fist into his hand. "If I find the punk who did this…"

"I'm thinking you should report this."

"You thinkin' the cops?"

"Definitely."

Todd stared off at the wall a moment. "I don't know." He took off his cowboy hat and scratched the top of his head. He turned the hat between his fingers a few times. "He's my brother and all that."

Alex nodded and set his laptop down on the coffee table. "These machines keep turning up in all the worst possible places."

"Speaking of worst possible places, how's work going?"

"I don't know. Our building burned to the ground the other night."

Todd's eyes grew large. "Was anybody hurt?"

"Nah. I was the only one there, but I got out. I'm thinking it was firebombed."

Todd put his hat back on his head. "Two big blows in two months. You okay, man?"

"Yeah. Hey, thanks for coming by."

"Not a problem."

"So where's Sean now?"

"I have no idea. He left with a bag. What gits me is I don't know where I went wrong. He used to be a good kid and all that. Then he started repeating my mistakes. Kid's making bigger ones all the time."

"Do you know if he had anything else of mine?"

"No idea. I don't think he had a clue who you were."

The two men remained silent a moment.

Alex motioned towards the kitchen. "Forgot to ask. Want anything to drink?"

"Pass. I have to get going, but I thought I'd let you know. Sorry about the office. If there is anything you need, gimme a jingle."

"Thanks. Hey, I have to ask you something. Why did you leave work?"

Todd stood up and cleared his throat. He hooked his thumbs onto the belt loops of his jeans and looked down at the coffee table a moment. "I didn't like where Pegasus was going."

Alex nodded, then smiled. "I hear ya. But it's over now."

"Why? Because the company burned down? If you really wanna know what's going on, keep on diggin'. You won't like what you find. I know I didn't. In fact, check out Lindemeier Consulting sometime. They're in downtown St. Paul. Lemme know if they're testing the hand chips yet."

"Hand chips?"

Todd made a tiny circle with his thumb and his index finger. "Yeah, little buggers like this. They sit on the back of your hand."

Todd then rounded the black iron railing between the living room and the stairs that led to the front door. He headed downstairs. Alex continued after him and opened up the front door.

"Wait. What do you mean I won't like what I find?" Alex asked.

"I mean it depends on how involved you wanna get." Todd tipped his cowboy hat a bit and stepped outside. "As for me, I'm done."

Alex followed him out onto the stairs. His friend then paced out to his white Mustang and climbed inside. The engine roared to life, and for a moment, Alex admired his friend's car.

As Todd backed out of the driveway, Alex surveyed the night. The moon shone down, full and bright, illuminating the driveway and something reflective near the edge of the asphalt. Thinking it was a piece of metal that would surely end up in his tire, he walked up to it and found it was a copper penny. He picked it up. As he turned it over between his fingers, he stared at the words arcing over Lincoln's portrait: In God We Trust. He pocketed the coin and reentered the house.

He marched back downstairs and entered the garage. The car still stunk a bit, and so he rolled down all four windows and turned on the carpet cleaner again. The machine was louder than a standard household vacuum cleaner, but the amount of grime and dirt it pulled out of the upholstery was remarkable.

A moment later he heard the hum of the automatic garage door and promptly banged his head on the roof of his car. He reached back and switched off the machine. He watched as Danielle pulled her car into the garage, and when he saw David wave to him from the backseat, a big grin broke across his face.

Alex rolled the carpet cleaner back towards the door to the house and unplugged it. The scent of wet carpeting, detergent, and smoke hung in the air as Danielle climbed out of the car and let David out of the backseat. Seconds later, Alex felt the python grip of his son's arms around his ankles.

Alex ruffled his son's hair and returned the hug. "How ya doin' buddy?"

"Great, Dad. I missed you."

"I missed you, too."

David ran over to Alex's car and tried to peer in through the driver's side window. "Eww. Yawr car stinks, Daddy."

Alex smiled as David then charged into the house and up the stairs. Danielle unloaded her suitcase from the trunk of her car and gazed longingly at Alex. He could see a spark again in her eyes—something that was missing days ago.

She strolled over to him and stood by him while he wrapped the power cord around his arm and lugged the machine inside. "It smells like smoke. You didn't take up smoking while I was away did you?"

"No. On Friday night, my workplace burned down."

Danielle dropped her suitcase on the ground, causing it to slam with a thud and topple over onto its side. As Alex hauled the machine and its sloshing contents through the doorway, she reached out a hand and felt his forehead.

"Are you okay? Were you at work?" Danielle said.

"Yes and yes. I climbed out through a window."

She put one hand to her mouth and the other on top of his head. Then he felt her hand discover a bump on his head. "Did you go see a doctor?"

"No need to. I'm alright."

He went into the laundry room, dumped the acrid, toxic-looking brew out of the carpet cleaner and then followed her upstairs. He then went back out into the garage and repeated the carpet cleaning process on the remaining seats in his car.

* * *

After Alex cleaned up, he sat down across from Danielle at the dining room table. She sorted through some receipts from her purse. She also had changed into a rather attractive pink nightgown and bathrobe, and let her hair down onto her shoulders.

"You are not going to like me. I picked up another shopping card from the grocery store," she said.

Alex drew back. "Why?"

"Alex, I really don't care if somebody discovers that I bought three boxes of facial tissue last week. Or some packs of light bulbs. Although I might want to hide my chocolate purchases."

He sighed and closed his eyes. "It's not that simple..."

"Sure it is. I don't do anything illegal. Do you? No. Case closed, then."

"Hold on. What if you end up in a lawsuit? What if they pull a bunch of your purchases up and use it as evidence? What if you buy a bottle of wine one day and they try to claim you are an alcoholic the next?"

"Alex, it's not like somebody sits around all day and digs through all that. Do they?"

"*I've seen the databases*. Ian pulled up some groceries he bought five years ago. Abernathy's is supposed to purge that information every three years."

He stared past her and at the fire now blazing in the fireplace. During the time he was downstairs, she apparently started one up. The folding brass and glass doors were pulled back, leaving only the iron screen as protection. He could feel the heat radiating out all the way across the room. It started to cause him to fall asleep at the table, until the hiss and pop of the wood startled him.

He watched her continue to work through her checkbook. Alex reflected a moment and then dove in. "Remember a few weeks ago when I got out of bed, went into the kitchen, and you checked in on me?"

She stopped writing in her checkbook and looked into his eyes. "I think so."

"Good. That was the night I heard a voice behind me. I think it was from the Lord. He said to go to Malloy and give him a message."

She looked off to the side with widened eyes and then back at Alex.

"It was strange," he said. "It was like I was ready to hear that."

"What do you think it means?"

"I'm not sure. I guess I'll found out." He glanced over at her purse. He noticed a green and blue Aspirizon Bank brochure sticking out, and the words "Liberty Cards" across the top. "Wait. You didn't get one of these cards from the bank, did you?"

"I'm thinking about it. Now what's wrong? Please don't tell me I can't have one of those, too. It's just a bank card. Besides, just because I pick up a brochure, doesn't mean…"

"It's not that. I have one already."

"Then what is it?"

"I don't know. I'm tired. I guess I'm thinking in circles now."

"I have some good news for us, Alex. I struck up a conversation with my brother, and he thinks he can get me a part-time position at his insurance office. I could start out as an administrative assistant. It's not what I want, but it probably beats a drill press job."

"Congrats. When do you start?"

"ASAP. Maybe even tomorrow. I'm so nervous, though."

"Why? You have a background in insurance."

"Here, come with me into the bedroom. I want you to help me pick out my outfit. I picked up a couple of new business suits at the mall. Maybe it's overdressing, I don't know. Maybe I should look at that drill press job again."

Alex rolled his eyes and stood up to follow her into the bedroom. Inside, he could feel the emotional exhaustion of the past few days starting to set in. It wearied his bones and made him feel as though he was trying to walk through a swimming pool filled with waist-deep water. He pushed his body forward, but knew within minutes of laying his head on the pillow for the night that he would be out for a good, long time.

"By the way, a co-worker of mine came over," he said as they arrived in their bedroom.

"And?"

"I found out who hit my account."

Chapter Twenty-Four

Four days later, Alex drove to downtown St. Paul in the middle of the day and parked inside of an hourly parking ramp. He then took the ramp elevator down two floors to the street level. The elevator's digital floor indicator chirped every time he went down a level. As soon as the elevator hit ground floor, the doors opened up to reveal a concrete stairwell and another doorway that led to the outdoors.

Already Alex could feel the bite of winter settling in, and as he pushed his way outside, his pulse accelerated. He zipped up his jacket further and braced himself from the cold wind that settled in now. The sky was gray and overcast, although the clouds on the horizon were white and fuzzy, as if they were about to unleash a torrent of snow.

He kept his eye on one particular building down the street. If one looked skyward, the pale brown stone exterior of the building housing Lindemeier Consulting appeared to be comprised of two different buildings, as if one was stacked on top of the other. The upper floors were cast in a dark brown brick, and from a distance it presented the illusion of a giant block built on top of rows of squared columns. An American flag jutted out of one side of the columns by the entrance, and the state flag of Minnesota sprouted out of the column on the opposite side.

He wove his way past several waiting passengers at a nearby bus stop. Nobody at the bus stop seemed to move out of his way, and so he continually calculated and recalculated the shortest path to his destination without stepping into the street. In minutes, he reached the building.

He pulled on the icy, metal door handle and stepped into the lobby. To his left was a long, low-to-the-floor wooden table with magazines splayed out in several directions. There were mauve chairs for waiting and the carpet was a dull red. Straight ahead was the security desk, which was nothing more than a fancy wooden desk with a swivel chair behind it. It was unoccupied for the moment.

Puzzled, he ventured to the elevators, and read a plaque on the wall listing the companies in the building. He scanned the list and found Lindemeier Consulting occupied the ninth floor. A businessman passed by him and entered an open elevator car. The man kept his hand in his pants pockets. He noticed Alex looking in his direction and held the elevator door open.

The man, who looked to be in his fifties, had gray, swept back hair, glasses, and a mustache. He was dressed in a light blue dress shirt without a tie and tan khakis.

"What floor?" The man said.

Alex ducked into the elevator. "Ninth."

The man hit the ninth floor button and waited for the doors to close. Alex hoped the man would reveal his right hand, so that he could see if he had a chip on the back of it. There was silence in the car until they reached the ninth floor, however.

When they reached the top, the man exited the elevator and walked up to a set of double glass doors with rounded steel handles. He swept the back of his hand against a black, playing-card-sized reader on the wall to gain access. He turned back to see Alex waiting. "Hi. Do you work here?"

"No. I'm going to Human Resources, though."

"Huh. I didn't realize we were hiring."

The businessman stared at him a moment as if to size him up. He noticed a cold, almost calculating presence about the man's face and especially in his eyes.

Alex felt beads of sweat forming on his palms and so he stuffed his hands in his pockets. He started to turn back towards the elevator. Then, the businessman broke the silence. "Well, cool. Nice to meet you. I'm Dave. You are?"

"Alex."

"Alex. Hmmm. Good luck, then."

"Thanks."

Alex followed the man through the doors. Dave took a left turn, while Alex headed in the opposite direction.

"Oh, Alex. HR is down this way. Down a couple cubes over from me," Dave said.

"Ah."

Alex followed Dave a moment and then turned down another row of large light-gray cubicles. The carpeting was a queasy deep brown, and over the head-high cubicle walls he could hear the ticking of computer keys that sounded like raindrops on pavement. He then passed by a set of cubicles with lower walls that were only waist-high. It looked to be a call center with chattering representatives wearing headsets and phones that chirped like electronic crickets.

After the call center, he passed more high-walled cubicles and was suddenly struck by a profound, muffled silence. Staring about, he did not see any type of reception desk.

"Over here, Alex," Dave said, as he pointed to the right.

Alex nodded and took the turn. He then approached the nearest occupied cubicle he could find. Inside, he found a woman in her mid-fifties, who had a yellow triangular mark on the back of her hand.

He spoke up. "Hi...I'm looking for Human Resources."

"Sure. It's over two cubes from me."

He then slipped up to a cubicle with the tag reading *Human Resources* on the outside wall. The black nameplate on an inside wall read *Connie Baker*. He noticed a woman sitting behind her computer, eating blueberry yogurt with a spoon, and reading something onscreen. Her cubicle was also filled with all sorts of plants, from small ferns to an aloe plant to the dozen bright red roses in a cylindrical vase on her desk. All these plus the two fake floor plants in the corners made him wonder if she harbored secret dreams of opening a floral shop someday.

He introduced himself. "Hi. My name is Alex Poole. I was, uh, wondering if you had any openings on your technology staff."

Connie, a Middle-Eastern woman with black curly hair, shot a fiery glance from her monitor towards Alex. "Openings? They should be listed on our intranet site." She narrowed her eyes and stared at him intensely. "Are you from down the floor somewhere?"

He stared at her right hand a moment and noticed a black, triangular mark on the back of it. It appeared to be slightly raised and perhaps held in place by some kind of adhesive.

"Well, I'm actually from outside the company. Say, I couldn't help but notice, but what is that on the back of your hand?"

Connie held out her right hand in front of her. "It's part of our security access system. You swipe your hand on the access plate and..."

Alex nodded and looked around her cubicle.

She crossed her arms and stood up suddenly. "Sir, do you have a contractor badge or some form of identification I can see?"

"Sorry, I followed another employee in. I probably should have called. Thanks."

Alex waved goodbye and left her cubicle. He charged back towards the front door. In seconds, he heard her start out of her cubicle and run after him.

In response, he began to run.

When he reached the exit, he rammed his way through the set of double glass doors and jabbed at the down button on the wall next to the elevator. The doors opened immediately. He jumped inside and turned to see her watching him from behind the glass doors. As the doors closed, a phrase came to his mind: *Go to James and speak to him, for his deeds have come up before me.*

He closed his eyes and took in a deep breath. The thought refused to leave him alone. He tried to shut it out by humming a few bars of a new Newsboys song heard a few weeks earlier. Then he tried to humor himself by pulling out his cell phone and playing a game of Breakout on it. When that did not work, he stared up and counted the tiles on the ceiling of the elevator.

In an instant, the elevator car bottomed out and the doors popped open. Three women and a man were waiting by the door, and now stared at him. All four had marks on the backs of their hands.

"Hi," he said, as his cheeks turned flush.

He dashed past the security guard desk, past the lounge chairs, and past the table full of magazines. Not turning to look back, he headed straight out the front doors of the building and back onto Fifth Street.

Chapter Twenty-Five

Once Alex was back on the street, he took a left and then another left around the corner of the building with the intention of returning to the parking garage. Something in his conscience, however, would not leave him alone.

Go to James...

Immediately, he tried to squelch the thought, but he knew in the end it would be useless. He walked the length of the building and then took a right and began to walk along Fourth Street. He continued to walk past the parking garage and on toward the Central Library. In his mind, he schemed up an e-mail to send out in haste to both Aspirizon Bank and Lindemeier Consulting.

Several blocks later, he arrived at the library. The Central Library was a large, multi-story building near the river and across from Rice Park. On the way inside the building, he thought about how he would use a public computer terminal, make up a temporary e-mail account, and send off an anonymous message. Yet, if the bank perceived the message as a threat, they would have its origins investigated, which could be traced back to the St. Paul public library, and ultimately, he figured, back to this terminal.

Would anybody present at the library remember him, though?

As he went through the metal detectors on either side of the entry doors, he surveyed his surroundings with a mixture of caution and nervousness. To his right was the Returns Desk, with its flowing counters, and to the left was the Checkout Desk. Ahead of him was the newly redesigned lobby with its gray walls, yellow signs, and brown flooring.

He took a deep breath to calm his nerves and realized that maybe this was all a mistake. In haste, he turned back around and returned to the street. A sudden surge of courage overcame him and he decided in that moment to meet James Malloy face to face.

* * *

After he returned to the parking ramp and paid the attendant, he drove to the bank headquarters. He made the drive in less than a half hour, and by the time he pulled into the parking lot of the headquarters, a light snow began to fall.

The headquarters stood like two giant, dark blue, upside-down, L-shaped glass blocks that would collapse in on each other if the supporting pillars near the front entrance were removed. The ten-story, blue block sections were connected in the middle by a section of topaz-colored glass that surely looked spectacular at sunset.

He stepped out of his car and ducked inside. Once in the lobby, it took him a minute to orientate himself. To the left, a series of open offices and burgundy lounge furniture beckoned customers. To the right, a curved teller counter greeted him, with black, smooth-flowing marble divided by mahogany walls. To the right of that on the wall, in brass lettering, read the words "Aspirizon Bank" in Century Gothic font.

Dashing straight ahead, he found the elevators at the end of a short, carpeted hallway. He entered an open car and jabbed at the tenth floor button. *What was he doing? Riding up to the corporate offices of Aspirizon Bank to tell James what?*

He stared at the mirrored walls of the elevator and checked his appearance. He felt a sudden surge of strength within his spirit as the elevator came to a stop. He stepped out of the elevator and onto the tenth floor, where the upper management offices resided.

There was little to greet him except a long, slender, black-tiled hallway and beige walls. At one end of the hallway stood a menacing set of double glass doors, behind which he could see a platinum-blonde administrative assistant on the telephone. Her back was turned towards him, and so he ran down the hallway up until she began to turn around. He then paced up slowly to the doors. He reached out and grabbed the door handle, which numbed his fingers like the icicles he used to grab off the roof as a kid. With one pull, he darted inside.

Putting his hands out on the reception desk, he burst into his speech the moment she hung up the phone. "I need to see your company president."

"Do you have an appointment?"

"No." Alex drummed his fingers on the desktop. "But it's urgent."

"You'll have to take a seat over there, sir. And your name please?"

"Alex. Alex Poole." He patted the cherrywood-topped desk and sat down.

To Alex, the administrative assistant looked to be in her mid-to-late thirties. She had a memorable set of blue eyes, slightly ruddy cheeks, and a narrow jaw line. She swept back a lock of her shoulder-length hair with her hand and picked up the telephone again. He tried to preoccupy himself with a copy of Field and Stream sitting on a nearby table. He noticed her watching him the entire time, however.

"Yes, he says he would like to see you," she said as she held the phone a moment. She called out to Alex. "What was your name again?"

"Alex Poole."

"His name is Alex Poole." She listened a moment and then nodded. "Oh. Okay."

She hung up the phone and stood up. "Mr. Malloy is willing to see you now. I'll lead you to his office."

Alex stood up and set the magazine back onto the table. He followed the assistant's lead through a series of short corridors. All the corridors had beige walls and black-tiled hallways like the hallway by the elevator. A faint scent of vanilla hung in the air. He also noticed several cameras scattered throughout the corridors and high up in the corners. They passed by many closed doors with security access boxes next to them.

After three turns, the administrative assistant swept a white identification badge against a black box near a set of double wooden doors. The nameplate next to the doors read "James Malloy, CEO."

She held the door open for him. He stepped inside and immediately felt something oppressive in the air. To his right were rows and rows of books in a set of oak bookcases. Straight ahead he could see a bank of windows, their blinds drawn up, and the snow continuing to fall gently outside. He then turned to see James Malloy standing up behind his desk.

"Thanks, Susan. You can leave us now," Malloy said.

Alex walked towards a set of three chairs that sat before Malloy's desk and reached out to shake Malloy's hand.

"Good to see ya, Alex. How are you?" Malloy said.

"Fine."

"Here. Sit down. What brings you up here?"

Alex sat down in the middle chair and gazed on at the cabinets to the right of Malloy, and then to the rock and roll poster to his left and finally at the rack of compact discs to the left of that. He began to think of a good reason for being here when suddenly a phrase came into his mind.

Forty days and you will be overturned.

He leaned back in his chair and cleared his throat.

"You okay?" Malloy said. "You look startled or something. Say, I heard about the fire at your workplace the other night. I just want to say it really breaks my heart to see something like that happen. If you have trouble finding work, I'm sure I can find an opening for you here."

Alex smiled weakly. "Thanks, but I don't think that's what I'm looking for right now."

A dead calm opened up between them. Malloy sat down in his chair and put his elbows on his desk. He appeared to be in deep thought about something or another. He reached for his glass candy jar on his desk and offered the jar to Alex. "Cinnamon bear?"

"No thanks."

Alex glanced over to the left of Malloy's desk to see a white Fender Stratocaster and an acoustic guitar side by side on two stands against the wall. "Why do you have guitars in your office?"

"Surprised? It beats a stupid plastic golf set on the floor any day. It helps me unwind, believe it or not. Gets the juices flowin'."

Malloy stared at Alex a moment. "Since you're here, I've got to show you something."

He stood up again and walked over to the Stratocaster which was sitting on a stand next to his rack of compact discs. "Check this out. I just learned this. By the way, I'd plug it in, but some of the other execs would probably freak if I started playing it too loud."

Malloy picked up the guitar and slipped the strap over his shoulder. He did not plug it into the amplifier, but instead began to strum out some opening notes of the song, *Hotel California*.

Alex grimaced and took a deep breath.

"What? You don't listen to that kind of music anymore?"

"No. Not anymore."

"How about this?"

Malloy began to strum out the opening bars of *My Woman From Tokyo*. "Remember that one?"

"I remember. But Jim, I'm not here for a job. I'm also not here for music lessons."

"Wait. Remember when we used to have lyric competitions? Yeah? I recited tons of songs verbatim."

Alex rolled his eyes.

"Oh. I get it. You've had another one of your Jesus moments."

"Jim, I have a message for you."

"Okay. Shoot."

Alex felt as if a big weight was now pressing down on his chest and shoulders. He felt the hair stand up on the back of his neck and on his arms. "I hate to tell you this, but the Lord says in forty days this place will be overturned."

Malloy stood motionless for what seemed like five minutes. He then burst into a fit of laughter. He continued to laugh as he slipped off his guitar strap. He set the guitar lovingly back onto its stand and composed himself. "Forty days, huh? Is that some kind of ultimatum?"

Alex squirmed in his chair now and felt his heart racing inside his chest like a car with a stuck accelerator pedal.

"I didn't say it. The Lord…"

"The Lord." Malloy pointed his index finger at Alex and shook his head in disapproval. "Alex, you're right. You don't need a job from me, you need a vacation. Do you have any savings stashed away?"

"I'm serious."

"Me too!"

"Well, uh…I've spent some time with my Bible lately and…"

Malloy looked as if he was struggling to restrain a laugh. "Man, I think you take the Bible way too seriously. C'mon. You and I both know it's a work of fiction. It's meant to be enjoyed like a fine wine or a great movie."

"Wait. No. I happen to believe otherwise…"

Malloy walked over to a window and stared out onto the streets below. "Listen, my Dad used to have these people come by the house.

Real holy rollers, ya know? But he'd take off with those kooks and their traveling carnival. They'd go on trips during the summer. Town to town. Leave us kids behind. That sorta stuff. Didn't make *one dent* in our hometown though. Still the same old cesspool today it always was…"

"I'm sure some people came to the…"

Malloy had both hands in the air now in an animated performance in front of the window. "Me, I dream big. I think big. Your God on the other hand gets all wacky if you so much as listen to the wrong kind of music. That's messed up."

Alex looked on at the poster behind Malloy's desk and then at the desk itself. He noticed two Matchbox cars on the corner of a blotter. On the floor before him he noticed a black, toy Model T laying on its side, perhaps because it rolled off. He knew Malloy had grandkids, so maybe it was from one of them. He bent down to pick it up and was going to put it back onto the desk, but instead held it inside his clenched fist. He could feel the anger rising in his chest the longer Malloy went on.

After a moment of holding the car in his fist, he decided to pocket it. He remembered as a child how another boy in his second grade class would steal things out of his desk—sometimes pencils, sometimes toy Matchbox cars. One day, Alex retaliated by swiping a toy car out of the other boy's desk. It was a game to him at that point in his life and one that brought a feeling of control and maybe even superiority.

Alex leaned back in his chair and then decided to stand up. "Jim," he said, "do you ever meddle with other people's accounts?"

Malloy spun around. "You really have changed haven't you? You've turned into a real piece of work." Malloy looked down at the floor and then at Alex. "Forty days and you'll be overturned, he says. This is coming from a guy who used to secretly swap cracked software?"

At that, Alex turned towards the door.

"Ah. You'd thought I'd forgotten that little tidbit from your past," Malloy said with a snarl.

"No. I gotta go."

Alex made several strides towards the door. He then lunged for the door handle and gave it a good tug.

"Yeah, go on, get out. Take a vacation and then talk to me."

All the way out into the hallway, through the corridors, through the double doors, and into the elevator, Alex's mind raced. The toy car in his pocket felt like molten metal burning a hole in his pants. Then, a nasty thought came into his mind.

Look at you. You're no better than you were before. Where's your redeemer now?

Alex thumbed the street level button in the elevator, but felt an urge to go back to the administrative assistant's desk. He looked on at the hallway from the elevator. Then, a reassuring thought came to him: *Go and steal no more.*

He held out his hand and stopped the doors from closing. He charged back into the hallway and down towards the double glass doors. With one quick motion he grabbed the door handle and marched up to Susan's desk. He pulled the toy car from his pants pocket. "Here, I found this on the floor in the back. Maybe someone will be looking for it."

He set the car onto her desk. Susan scrunched her eyebrows together and pursed her lips. He then turned back towards the double glass doors. In that moment, he felt as if the giant weight on his chest had been lifted off of him for good.

Chapter Twenty-Six

The elevator bottomed out at street level. Alex stepped out into the hallway and looked around. To his right were several revolving doors that led outside. To his left was the bank lobby. Although he wanted to make it easy on himself and bolt outside, he figured it might be wiser to close down his account and then bolt.

He marched back over to the bank lobby and stood in line. He glanced around and behind him, continually checking back towards the elevators for any signs of security or Malloy himself. Along the curved, black, marble teller counter, he counted four out of six open teller windows and eight silver-tube cameras along the top part of the back wall. Each teller was dressed in a crisp, white shirt and black pants, almost as if they were running a casino.

He also noted a security guard sitting at a desk near the front door of the building. The guard then turned towards Alex and said something into the radio that was strapped onto his shoulder.

A minute later, a teller window opened up. The teller smiled as Alex stepped forward. She was a tall Hawaiian woman in her early twenties with long, jet black hair and a mole to the right of her nose. "Good afternoon sir. How can I help you?"

"Hi. I'd like to close my account."

"Aw, sorry to hear that. Do you have some proof of identification and your account number?"

He slid his checkbook across the black marble counter along with his driver's license.

The teller stared at his license a moment and immediately began clicking away at her keyboard. She stared at her screen a moment and then slid the license back. She swept her hair back over her shoulder with her hand.

"Alex, I see here you've only been with us two months or so. Is there any particular reason why you are not staying with us?"

"I just would really like to close my account."

"But sir, if you'd like, I could have you sit down with a banker and they could discuss some options with you."

"No. That's alright."

"Sir, we also offer several types of accounts. We have low interest checking, free checking…"

"Please. No. I just want to close it. Today."

Alex could feel his temperature rising. Again he checked behind him, looking toward the elevators and then back at the guard desk. The guard looked down a moment at something or another and then stared in Alex's direction again. He was a burly, balding man with a white, handlebar mustache. There looked to be absolutely no sense of humor in the man's eyes.

"Okay, Alex. If you insist. But you won't find a better deal elsewhere. May I ask who you are going with instead?"

"I don't know yet."

"Well, your balance is nine hundred and fifty seven dollars and twelve cents."

Alex nodded.

The teller tore off a pink and white document from a printer beneath the counter. She slid it across the counter for him to sign. He snapped up a black and gold pen that was chained to the counter and signed his name on the signature line. When he finished, he handed the forms back to her and watched her separate them.

"Would you like that in cash or as a cashier's check?" She said.

"Cash works. Hundreds please."

The teller began to count out the bills into a neat pile before him on the polished marble counter. As soon as the last of the coins hit the counter he scooped up the pile and left as fast as he could. On the way out the door, he saw the security guard eyeing him. The guard moved out from behind his desk and so Alex accelerated his pace until he cleared the exit doors.

He resisted the urge to look back.

On his way to the car, he shoveled the cash into his wallet. He had no clue where he was going to put his money next and surely Danielle would freak out if he started to stuff hundred dollar bills underneath their mattress. Bills still needed to be paid and his mind began to flip through the possibilities of where to bank next.

He climbed into his car and left the parking lot with a squeal of his tires. He took a deep breath and made fast for the freeway. For several blocks, he checked his rearview mirror and only when he was several blocks away did he turn on his car radio. He jabbed at the station buttons and decided on a familiar station to settle his nerves.

Then he heard the ending lines of the song *Big Fish*.

At that he killed the radio with the off button.

* * *

An hour passed before James Malloy settled back into his desk chair. The phone rang twice since Alex's departure, and then a couple executives from down the hall pestered him for a good half hour about the ongoing bank fire investigation. After he drove them out of his office, he took a deep breath and muttered to himself.

In front of his computer screen now, he decided to find some answers. He pulled up Alex's account number on VIPR, one of Aspirizon's mainframe account systems. What he saw next on his screen only made him angrier.

According to VIPR, Alex apparently had closed his account sometime today, either before or after his little "forty days" stunt. No matter. He peeked over at the cross reference from Alex's VIPR account to the LCTS mainframe system and found Alex also owned a Liberty Card at some point. He picked up his phone and called Susan into his office.

A minute later Susan walked in. Malloy leaned back in his chair and put his hands behind his head and grinned.

She stood in front of his desk holding something in her left hand. "Yes?"

"You remember that man we let in here about an hour ago?"

"Of course."

"Maybe you didn't know this, but he used to be my employee years ago at the bank."

Susan sat down in the middle chair opposing Malloy. She continued to hold onto something or another in her hand.

"Anyway, the guy comes up here, and we talk a bit and I even offer him a job. Get this—a job. Most anywhere in the company. Then he goes on to tell me the real reason he's here. He says, 'I hate to tell you this, but the Lord says in forty days this place will be overturned.' I busted out laughing. What a piece of work."

Susan's eyes widened and then she began to stare at the floor. And at the walls. And at the windows.

"Something wrong, dear?" Malloy said.

Susan stood up and reached out her left hand and dropped the toy Model T onto his desk. It hit the desk with a clunk and did a couple of rolls to land on its side. "This is what he gave to me on the way out."

Malloy picked up the car and twirled it between his fingers. "Hmm. I was wondering where that little bugger went. It was from one of the grandkids." He set the car back onto his desk next to the other ones. "Here, come over here and look at this."

Susan stood still a moment. Malloy waved her on a few times.

"Here. Check this out." He pulled up Alex's account information again and then his Liberty Card information. He then pointed his finger to a lone entry in the Liberty Card transaction log which showed a purchase from Abernathy's Liquor Store. "The guy's a bona fide Jesus kook but drinks booze, then takes something of mine, and has the nerve to threaten me. I'll have to come up with an answer to that."

Susan backed away from the terminal, and stared at the floor again. She began to creep towards the security doors.

"Before you go, I want you to find someone to run me a report that cross checks those LAMPS kooks with LCTS. We can't be too careful," he said.

"Lamps?"

"Yeah, yeah. There's a group that's been bothering the crap outta me lately." He opened up his desk and pulled out a tan-colored brochure. "Ever seen one of these brochures? They've sent protesters out front before, too. The whole lot of 'em are a piece of work."

Susan continued on towards the door and did not stop until she pulled on the door handle.

"Oh, and Susan, are you okay? Usually you're much more talkative."

She glared back at him and then left the room without another word.

Malloy shook his head and swore. He slammed his desk drawer shut and rubbed his chin. He puttered with the Model T a moment, then pulled a letter opener out from another desk drawer. He took the top envelope from his inbox pile and slit it open. Out fell a letter and a brochure from a local theater company. The letter solicited funds and sponsorship, while the brochure covered the upcoming theater season. The brochure mentioned that from November to late December, the theater was putting on a production of *A Christmas Carol*.

Inside there was also a note about some of the theater members going caroling on a couple of dates during the holidays. Although he generally was only mildly annoyed by them, he did remember one song as a kid that would always cause him to crack somehow, but he never knew why.

What was it?

Oh yes.

Something, something. La, la, la, la, la, la...la, la, la, la...in Excelsis Deo!

Whatever that meant.

* * *

Across town and hours later under cover of the dark, Ben pulled a small trailer behind his car into an alley. The alley ran behind an abandoned warehouse on the edge of Bloomington and was covered now with a couple of inches of fresh snow. In the summer, decaying weeds ringed the perimeter of the faded-white warehouse, which was a long, two story building with windows every twenty feet and a navy blue roof. Ben noted earlier in the summer how the property passed through several realtors' hands.

He parked his car, killed the engine, and doused his lights. With a bolt cutter, a crowbar, and a flashlight in hand, he snuck up to a back entrance door marked "Deliveries" and cut the cheap padlock off the door. The lock hit the ground with a dull thud. He opened the door and shone a flashlight around a mostly empty interior storage room. In a corner of the room, however, were several dark blue tarps covering something. After looking back down the alley one last time, he crept inside.

He walked over to the tarps and peeled them back. There were a dozen or so unopened cardboard cartons, each marked with the words "casement window" on the side. With a final sweep of the flashlight, he analyzed the remainder of the room. When he was finished, he hustled back to the door, for he knew he had found the perfect hiding place. It was also the perfect building since it was midway between his mother's house and his ultimate target.

Perfect for a revolution of sorts.

Outside, he looked around the alley again, then peeled back the black tarp on his trailer. Underneath the tarp was a red moving dolly and three small drums of gasoline. One by one, he wheeled each drum inside, followed by several unmarked wooden crates. As a final covering, he hauled in the black tarp and secured it over the crates and the drums.

He walked around the room for a minute and noticed a doorway that led to another room. On any other night he would have explored the building in full. Tonight, however, he made haste and left the building.

Ben pulled another padlock out of his pocket and secured the delivery door. He scampered back to his car and strapped the dolly back onto the trailer. In less than two minutes, he was gone.

Chapter Twenty-Seven

On Saturday afternoon, Alex sat on the sofa, fanning through a fresh ream of white, twenty-pound bond paper with his fingers. Printouts of the pages from Aspirizon's bank website already covered the sofa and carpet beneath his feet. Intermingled with those pages were articles printed from the LAMPS website. Piles of library books on finance, identity theft, and circuit design weighed down the coffee table in front of him like an impending avalanche.

He glanced down to spot the edges of a resume and a list of personal references at the bottom of one of the stacks. Crumpled resumes, a classified section with orange highlighter marks and two empty bottles of Mountain Dew littered the floor. He fed the printer attached to his laptop, rubbed his weary eyes and looked over at his opened Bible on the end table next to the recliner.

Minutes later he heard the familiar sound of the electric garage door opener, heralding the arrival of Danielle and David from the mall. He got up off the sofa to stretch his legs and for the first time in hours, noticed it was snowing heavily outside. As the printer brr-brr-brred through another page, he eyed the snow shovel in the corner by the front door.

Danielle and David bounded up the steps soon after that. As Danielle unloaded a couple of plastic bags onto the kitchen counter, David bolted off into his bedroom. Alex returned to the sofa and started to look over the printouts. A moment later, he felt Danielle's hand on his shoulder. With the other hand she held out a bank card in front of Alex's face.

"Guess what I got," she said. "Do you have one of these?"

Alex reached out and took the card from her hand. He held it close to his eyes. On the front of the card was the familiar green and blue Aspirizon logo along with the words "Liberty Card" in blue lettering. There was no usual magnetic stripe on the back of the card, however.

He cringed as she pulled the card back from his grasp.

"What's wrong?" She said. "Mine just arrived in the mail. They had a holiday special on them. *I'm a preferred customer now.*"

"Figures. Right before Thanksgiving, too. Let me see that card again."

Danielle thrust it out to him, then playfully pulled it away.

"Not funny."

"Don't be so paranoid. Besides I get bonus points for purchases."

Alex closed his eyes a moment. "Danielle, I didn't tell you this but a couple of days ago, I dumped my Aspirizon account. You might want to follow suit."

She waltzed around the sofa and stood in front of him with her hands on her hips. "What? Why?"

"Those bonus points mean they're tracking you, too."

Danielle rolled her eyes.

"Danielle, do you remember what I told you about the message I received a few weeks back? And how I said that it seemed like God wanted me to talk to Malloy?"

"Yes. No. You didn't…"

"I did. I walked into Malloy's office and told him."

"What did you tell him?"

"In forty days his place would be overturned."

Danielle closed her eyes and rubbed her temples with her right hand. "I need to sit down."

"He laughed at me when I told him."

"Remember what I said before about seeing you two confront each other? Forget I said that."

David came down the hallway at this time and zoomed two F-16 plastic fighter jets through the living room airspace. He then turned to fly downstairs. He stopped halfway down the stairs, however. "Mommy, are you okay?"

"Yes, dear."

"You got headache?"

"Yes. Mommy's going to need an aspirin."

"I'll get it."

"No, no, David. Mommy will get it. Better yet, Daddy will get it if Daddy wants to sleep in his own bed tonight."

Alex stood up, as if on cue. "I do like to sleep in my own bed," he said in a sarcastic voice. He walked into the bathroom and pulled out the Tylenol bottle, and returned to the living room. David continued his flight downstairs.

Danielle took the bottle from Alex and stood up to get some water from the kitchen. "I'm surprised he laughed at you. At least he didn't have you arrested or anything like that. What happened after that? Do I wanna know?"

Alex shrugged his shoulders. "Then I went downstairs and closed my account. End of story. So far."

"Let's hope no one prints up tee shirts for you."

"At least I went all out."

"You went all out alright."

He walked back over to the coffee table and pulled out the LAMPS brochure Kay gave him weeks ago. "I was thinking. I reread this and checked out the LAMPS site. There's some good articles on there. They're even having a rally in a couple days."

"You're not thinking of…"

"I am. I want to go. I want some answers. I want to know who tried to kill me."

"What makes you think they know anything about that?"

"I want to make sure it's not them. Or if it is them, confront them."

"What's come over you lately? All of a sudden you're picking fights."

"Hey, I'm just the messenger."

"What's the maximum safe dose of Tylenol I can take?"

"Seriously. They're having a pre-rally organizational meeting this evening."

"Alex, it's a blizzard outside. Why don't you let the investigators handle things?"

"But look, it's just down the road. A couple of miles maybe. Okay, five."

"Did you spend any time looking for jobs today?"

He stuffed his hands into his jeans pockets and stared on at the coffee table and the sofa, and then at the crumpled resumes on the floor. He picked one of them up and paraded it into the kitchen. "See? Look. There's one off the floor."

"What good does it do on the floor? You're supposed to mail them, not use them for basketball practice."

"I have to get them right before I mail them."

Danielle wandered over to the dining room window and pulled back one of the beige curtains. "Alex, it's snowing even harder out there now. It's a whiteout."

"It's not a whiteout. You're exaggerating. I want to know who tried to take me out. Know what? You're welcome to come with. In fact, *I want you to come with.*"

"I can't. I've got some letters I want to write tonight."

He shrugged his shoulders again and began to pick up the papers off the sofa and the floor. "Tomorrow's Sunday. Write your letters then."

She returned from the kitchen with a cup of water and a pair of scissors. Then she picked up her Liberty Card and turned to face Alex. "This thing creeps you out, doesn't it?"

"A few things in tech creep me out. That's a special kind of creepy. Hey, did I tell you about my visit to Lindemeier consulting? Some of their employees had chips on their hands."

She stood for a moment in silence. Then: "Do you want me to do the honors or should I?"

"You're going to cut it up?"

"Sounds like the best thing to do."

She clasped the card with one hand and the scissors with the other. She squeezed the handles with enough visible force to break the scissors in half. One half of the card dropped to the floor.

Alex picked up the half that was lying on the carpet and examined it. Inside he could barely make out a thin layer of some type of silver or metallic foil. "Cute. This one's better than the one I had. Lucky you."

As Danielle tossed her half into the kitchen garbage can, he continued to pick up the papers off the sofa and closed his laptop. "Does this mean I can go?"

* * *

An hour later after dinner, Alex drove up Century Avenue in a near blizzard to Highway 94. He then crept along the highway, towards White Bear Avenue. Along the way, he counted two cars on the shoulder, one spinout, and two tow trucks in transit. His car never went above twenty miles per hour until he reached White Bear Avenue.

On that same freeway he also saw a billboard that seemed to encourage him. It was a dark blue billboard with all sorts of words and phrases scattered about in multiple colors. The words and phrases included fear, job loss, depression, anxiety and uncertainty. There, in the middle of all the words, was a larger phrase that asked, "How big is your God?" At the bottom of the billboard it read: Isaiah 40:13. He decided he would commit that to memory and look it up later.

He eventually took an exit onto White Bear Avenue and then turned onto a side street until he located Brian's house. The snow was cast in an eerie, orange streetlight glow. Several snow-covered cars sat out in front of his small, pine-green rambler, and all the house lights appeared to be on. The yard appeared sparse, with only a pair of tall, snow covered evergreens on either side of the front door and a row of hedges along one part of the sidewalk.

He slipped out of his car and put up the hood on his black-and-gray Columbia jacket. He then walked headfirst into the driving snow and plodded his way up the driveway to the front door. He rung the doorbell and waited.

Kay opened the front door ten seconds later. "Alex! What are you doing here?"

"I read up on your meeting. Got room for one more?"

"Of course."

Once inside he stomped the snow off his sneakers onto a black welcome mat and surveyed the room. The house had extensive hardwood flooring and the kitchen and dining room areas were cluttered. The living room had two plush, dark brown couches and a matching recliner. A large throw rug with a lakeshore scene sat on the living room floor, and on the coffee table in front of one of the couches were several kerosene lantern parts and an open manual.

He caught a glimpse into one the side bedrooms. He could see a professional-looking microphone stand and possibly some recording equipment, as it if were part of a homemade recording studio. He remembered how Brian posted professional-sounding podcasts on his website.

Six people were gathered around the dining room table, poring over diagrams and paperwork. In the middle of it all sat somebody's orange alley cat, basking in the attention.

Kay took Alex's jacket and hung it in the hallway closet. She then went around the table and introduced everyone. It took a moment for Alex's eyes to adjust from the snowy outdoors to the brightly lit room. At first, everything looked washed out and even a bit pink.

"And you know Brian, my brother. This is one of our newest members, Ben. And my old friend Becca from high school."

Alex waved to each of them in turn and for once noticed Brian was actually smiling. In fact, he even pulled out a folding chair for Alex. "Welcome, my man, welcome. What brings you out on a dumpy night like this?"

"Questions. News. Updates."

"Let's hear the news."

Kay interrupted their banter. "By the way everyone, this here's Alex. He's a software engineer at Hoyle-Aspen."

"Was. Which brings me to the news. My workplace burned down," Alex added.

Alex noticed Kay and Brian's eyes widened like saucers. "I hope nobody here had anything to do with that."

"Oh gosh, Alex, no." Kay put a hand on his shoulder and looked him straight in the eye. "Honest, we had nothing to do with that. Are you okay? Was anybody hurt?"

"I'm fine. I made it out okay. But whoever it was they threw something into the office next to me. The place lit up in minutes. I had to go through a window to get out."

"I read about the fire online," came Brian's reply.

Alex scanned the rest of the faces around the room, but no one gave anything away. Then, Ben cleared his throat. Alex eyed him carefully, noting his blonde, surfer-like hairstyle and his midnight-blue shirt with the molecular structure of caffeine emblazoned in white across the front of it. There was a peculiar, calculating presence in the man's eyes, almost like the businessman he saw in the elevator at Lindemeier Consulting.

"Have they figured out who did it?" Ben said.

"Not that I know of. But I haven't heard from the investigators lately," Alex replied.

"Were they able to save anything?"

"Not much. The server room went up in minutes. I was too busy dodging burning tiles on the way to save much."

"Fire must have gone through the ceiling then. Did you see if…"

"Ben, let's discuss something else," Kay said, looking over at Alex, then back at Ben.

Ben put up two open hands and backed away a bit from the table. To Alex, he almost seemed to be struggling to conceal a smile.

Then Brian spoke up again. "Yeah, let's give the man a rest. Sounds like you've been through hell anyway. So what updates do you have?"

Alex leaned back in his folding chair and smiled. "Ever do any research on Aspirizon Bank?"

"Some. Why?"

"I dropped them as my bank. I also confronted the president about a couple of things. Any of you bank there?"

Only Becca spoke up. "My Mom does. I think."

"She might wanna pull out. Now I don't have definitive proof yet, but I was doing some research and talking with some friends and I started to put some pieces together."

Alex stood up and returned to the coat closet by the front door and pulled out a roll of printed articles and notes fastened together by a rubber band. He returned to the table and the cat, startled, jumped to the floor. He unrolled his papers and set them in the middle of the table. He noticed Ben continuing to stare on at him.

"This top sheet is an example of what my company used to do. We made prison bracelet and house arrest systems. Real good ones, too. But I found out kind of late that Aspirizon's president was interested, too. Way too interested. Seems he somehow hooked up with one of our sales guys and then the sales guy started peddling a retail version. Then…"

Alex pushed aside the Pegasus diagram and showed them a sketch of what he remembered from his visit to Lindemeier Consulting. "…I visited a place in St. Paul where some employees were wearing these. So I did some follow-up research. I found more connections to Aspirizon. I also found out that the chips use some kind of thin disc or triangle that rests on the back of your hand. It's worthless when removed."

He then flipped to the next piece of paper which was a photocopy of a newspaper article. "But get this. Somebody has already attempted to hack it. So they encased the chip in some kind of dark film material to protect it from something called a 'Shelby attack'. Some scientist in a lab shot a laser at the original version and found out he could disable its defenses in less than ten seconds."

Kay crossed her arms and leaned forward over the table and the diagrams. "Ben, tell him about your relative."

Ben grimaced and to Alex it looked like he wanted to excuse himself from the room.

Kay egged him on. "Go on, Ben."

Ben sighed. "I have a relative in prison in Wisconsin. He's uh…having to deal with the prison bracelet system," he said in a heavy Southern accent.

"Ah. Walworth, I take it?" Alex replied.

"Yeah."

An uneasy silence swept through the room. Brian spoke up. "I was just thinking about how all this fits in with the cluster plans we found."

"Cluster plans?" Alex said.

"Right. We found out that the bank and several others were working on massive data tracking and storage facilities spread out across several cities. We think Chicago, Minneapolis, Detroit, St. Louis, Philadelphia and Dallas for starters. Not sure what is up with that."

Brian then pointed to a large map of the United States that was spread out on the table before them. Several cities were marked off on the map with red dots.

Ben suddenly became visibly agitated. He clapped his hands together and stood up. "I got it. Here's what we should do. We should protest at their branches. Maybe their headquarters. Make a really bold statement. I betcha they'll back down then."

Brian leaned back on his barstool and crossed his arms. "What kind of protest were you thinking of?"

"Signs. Pickets. If that doesn't work, escalate. Let 'em know we mean business."

Kay crossed her arms. "No, we're a peaceful group. We don't need to get arrested. Besides we've picketed there before. I don't know if it mattered. We're kind of in a precarious position."

"Ah. You won't get arrested."

A couple of the members at the table whispered amongst themselves.

"I think the rally on Monday will be sufficient. Besides we still don't have enough hard proof. Writing letters might be better," Kay added after a moment of thought.

Alex's cell phone rang. He stepped towards the front door to look at the screen. According to the display, his old boss Drew was calling. He let the call go to voicemail. At the same time, he realized it was time to get going. He reached into the coat closet to grab his jacket and then returned to the table. He picked up his articles and diagrams off the table and rolled them back up neatly.

"Leaving so soon?" Brian said.

"My wife's gonna worry."

"Will we see you Monday?"

"I'll think about it."

Alex waved to everyone and meandered towards the door. Something bugged him about Ben, but he could not figure it out. As he left out the front door, Kay followed him onto the front steps.

"Thanks for coming," she said.

"Thanks for standing up. Hey, uh, I had a question for you. I was rereading a passage out of Revelation earlier today. Chapter thirteen, verses sixteen and seventeen, I think. I know you guys are all hung up on the economic angle of this. But don't you think it's more of a worship thing with the mark?"

"You've really been thinking this through, haven't you?"

Alex nodded in agreement. "What's up with that Ben guy, by the way? He kept staring at me."

"He's new. We've had some new members lately." Her voice trailed off.

"You make it sound like that's a bad thing."

"They seem like they're stirring things up."

"That's bad?"

"It is if it involves violence."

"Can't you kick the troublemakers out?"

Kay sighed as Alex continued towards his car. "We're making an attempt to do that."

Alex looked up to notice the snow stopped falling. He pulled out his cell phone and dialed home. He waved towards Kay, who then went back inside. When his wife answered he spoke up. "Danielle? Hey, it's me. I'm on my way home."

After he climbed into his car he looked over at the Bible that he brought with him. He opened it up on the passenger seat and found the verse from Isaiah he saw on the billboard earlier. It read: *Who has understood the mind of the Lord, or instructed Him as His counselor?*

Chapter Twenty-Eight

Two days later, after Danielle left for work and David left for school, Alex ventured to the rally, which was held at one in the afternoon. He parked his car in a ramp on Washington Avenue several blocks away from the Northrop Mall on the Minneapolis Campus of the University of Minnesota. The moment he stepped out of the parking ramp and arrived onto street level, he could begin to hear the chanting of the crowd and the distant echoes of a public address system.

He crammed his hands into his pockets. The words of the speaker became clearer and Alex surmised that it might even be Brian's voice, more animated than he had ever heard, and crackling as time went on. Another thunderous round of applause went up as Alex forged his way down Washington Avenue, through crowds of students with backpacks commuting between classes.

Years elapsed since he attended school here and only a few external building changes seemed evident. At once the campus felt familiar again, and memories flooded back to him now of crisscrossing the grounds to get to his classes, bumping into transitory friends and standing in endless lines to sign up for classes. He remembered how he dated a couple of women he met in his classes, yet somehow he never got the hang of campus life entirely, although he lived in a dormitory for two years.

After passing the black and red brick Electrical Engineering building and upon reaching Ford Hall, he rounded the corner and began down towards the gathering on the Mall. In his estimation, he counted around three hundred people, maybe more, and he could not see the speaker. A few students stood on and gawked from a distance, and Alex imagined the professors conducting classes up and down the Mall were probably hoping for more snow. The sun was out, however.

The Mall stretched between Northrop Hall on the north and Washington Avenue on the south, and in the summer from the air it looked like a large rectangle of grass, bordered by several campus buildings and sidewalks. The rectangle itself was split into strips by even more sidewalks. On the four corners of each strip were knee-high hedges. Large trees loomed over the sidewalks, as globular streetlamps and marble benches lined the walkways themselves. On the grass strip before Northrop's outdoor plaza, near the towering façade of Walter Library, Alex spied the bulk of the protesters.

As he crossed the Mall, he peeked above the heads of the gathered crowd to view the speaker. Brian stood on a makeshift wooden stage before a microphone and a set of speakers, wearing a black jacket and a black stocking hat. A white and green LAMPS banner was draped across the front of the stage. In his hand, he held up an Aspirizon Bank brochure. For a moment, Alex felt the urge to turn right around and slip back between the buildings and disappear.

Brian then waved some type of plastic bracelet over his head and jabbed his finger back towards the crowd. "This! This is what we are heading towards. Is this the future we want to turn over to our children?"

"No!" Someone in the crowd shouted back.

Alex grimaced and began to turn back towards the parking ramp. That is, until a woman reached out and grabbed him by the arm.

"Alex?" She said.

It was Kay. She wore blue jeans and a canary yellow ski jacket. Along with that, she sported a pale blue stocking hat and matching gloves. She rested a hand on his shoulder. "It's good to see you. How are you doing?"

"I'm fine. I know you told me before what you think of violence. Your brother sounds a little keyed-up there on stage."

Kay bit her lower lip. "Well, nobody's perfect. It's something he's passionate about alright. These events are always an adventure."

"I know...I've listened to a sample of his podcasts a couple times. He's a real card."

He scanned the crowd for Ben, thinking surely he would attend something like this. Instead it looked as if he was no where to be found.

They turned their attention back towards Brian on the stage, who was doing an admirable job of whipping the crowd up into a frenzy. To Alex, the crowd seemed nonviolent. He then saw Brian glance in their direction. Brian thrust a finger towards Alex. Alex's eyes darted towards the ground but it was too late.

"Alex! Alex! Come up here a moment!" He heard him yell into the microphone. "Friends, there is a man in the back who knows exactly what is going on. Alex, come up here!"

He turned towards Kay. "No, I'm not going up there. I don't do well in front of crowds."

She tried to wave Brian off. Alex then took the opportunity to elbow his way through the crowd. By now several students had gathered behind Alex, and by his guess, it meant another ten bodies deep to wade through. Brian persisted in calling his name, and Alex felt his cheeks becoming flush, as he watched several people stare at him.

He continued to press onward towards his car. He considered stopping at the Village Wok restaurant down the street before heading home. He craved sweet and sour chicken anyhow.

Suddenly, he found his way blocked by a Korean student carrying a shoebox full of small wooden crosses. The man held out one to Alex. "Would you like a cross, sir?"

"Sure. Thanks."

"Peace and grace to you."

"Thanks. You, too."

Alex cradled the wooden cross between his fingers. There was nothing remarkable about it and on the top was a metal loop. Through the metal loop was strung a piece of cherry red yarn. He witnessed the man with the crosses continue on his way, handing one out to all who wanted them. Alex noted Kay taking one as he turned back towards the direction the parking ramp.

* * *

After stopping for some lunch, Alex drove by the snow-covered ruins of Hoyle-Aspen. The remainder of the building stood unharmed, but the blackened remains of his workplace begged for demolition. Yellow police tape fluttered in the wind, strung from tree to tree. He parked his car in the parking lot and walked up to the outer perimeter of tape.

He tried to catch a glimpse of his office, and instead saw into Drew's office. His bookcase was still there, volumes soaked, selected books gone, and some blackened or ashen. On the grayed wall behind Drew's desk a clear oval could be seen right where his mounted fish used to hang. Smirking at the moment, Alex spied red spray-painted dashes on the sidewalk and the asphalt before him in the parking lot.

Several paces back towards his car, he imagined the location of the arsonist, the arc of the firebomb took and the tinkle of the glass as it smacked into the window of the Charles' office. Then he remembered the odd hissing sound he heard before the glass broke. For a moment, he wondered if it was instead some kind of rocket that was fired at him.

He glanced at his watch. David would be home from school soon. He returned to his car and pulled out the wooden cross from his jacket pocket. Something bothered him about it. He stared at it closely, and noticed it was made of two halves glued together. *Was there something wrong in the way the man said "peace and grace to you?"*

He grabbed his Bible from the backseat and opened it. He read several opening verses from many of Paul's letters in the New Testament. He checked Philippians, Ephesians, Galatians, Romans and both the Corinthian letters. They all included the words "Grace and peace to you" not "peace and grace to you."

Maybe it was nothing, he thought.

Chapter Twenty-Nine

A little over a week later, Alex stood in his kitchen, holding the refrigerator door open, brooding over its contents. He noticed a half-gallon carton of orange juice appeared to have leaked out onto the bottom, for there were drippings on the bottom shelf of the fridge. He cleaned it out, and pulled open the crisper drawer. There lie the six pack of canned beer he had forgotten about.

None of the cans were missing, although one was detached of course. He bent down and pulled out the cans and set them on the counter. One by one he popped them open and poured them down the drain. The beer made the sink stink and so he flushed the smell out with soap and water. He tossed the cans into the recycling bucket in the corner. He recalled how it was one of the few purchases he made with his now defunct Liberty Card.

A few minutes later, he went downstairs and opened the front door. He watched David jump off the bus and charge across the snow and up to the front door. His son was wearing a dark blue winter jacket with matching snow pants, a black stocking hat, and mittens.

Alex opened the door and gave his son a bear hug. "How was your day, buddy?"

"Good. Dad, can I get the mail?"

Alex smiled and helped his son take off his black, red, and yellow Spiderman backpack. "Sure. Can you reach up that high?"

David jumped up off the floor. "Yeah."

Alex let David out the front door again and watched from the front steps as his son scurried down the driveway. It was a cloudy day and a few flurries began to bumble their way out of the heavens now.

David reached into the mailbox and immediately pulled out a stack of advertisements and what looked like junk mail. A few pieces dropped to the ground. Then, Alex noticed that he kept on pulling out more mail.

And even more mail after that.

A heavy feeling settled into Alex's stomach as he watched his son struggle under the load. He ran down the driveway to help.

"Lots of mail, Daddy," David said.

"There is."

David handed the mail to his father. He picked up more pieces off the ground and brushed the snow off of them before handing them over, too. Meanwhile, Alex checked inside the mailbox and pulled out a phone bill.

David looked at some of the ads still in his hands. "What's this word? B-e-e-r."

"Here I'll take that."

Alex began to leaf through what appeared to some type of microbrewer's supply catalog. Then he noticed another similar catalog. And another.

Then he found several unmarked white envelopes addressed to him with no return address. Each postmark was from a different state. He sighed as David bounded up the front steps and held the door open for his father.

They both dumped the mail into one big pile on the dining room table. Alex counted twenty-five pieces in all, and threw out the beer supply catalogs immediately. He then sat down and tore open the first unmarked envelope he picked up. David, meanwhile, ran into his room to play.

Inside the envelope was a lone piece of paper with a listing of several dozen account numbers and names. In shock, he tore the paper to bits and threw it into the garbage. Against his better judgment he tore open two other envelopes and found more names and account numbers inside of them.

In one swift motion, he swept the unmarked envelopes off the table and into the trash. He dreaded to think what would arrive in the mail tomorrow.

A few seconds later, the metallic ding-dong of the doorbell sent Alex upright in a hurry. He tore down the stairs and lunged for the front door. A young, thin man in his mid-twenties greeted him. Dressed in a white dress shirt, a black business suit, and a dark blue tie, he spoke with a heavy English accent. In his hand was a book, but it did not appear to Alex to be a Bible.

"Good afternoon, sir," he said. "I'm traveling throughout your neighborhood on behalf of one of the churches in the area and was wondering if I could share something with you that just might change your life."

As the man spoke, Alex felt an unfamiliar force nearby, almost as if some invisible hostile hand pressed against his chest. His heart pummeled itself against his ribcage, and he felt sweat beginning to form around his collar. He felt the urge to run. "I'm kind of busy right now, and…"

"We're all busy, I'm sure, but some things should not wait."

Snowflakes tumbled out of the sky, dotting the shoulder's of the man's coat. Alex noticed the man trying to peer around his shoulders and glance inside the house.

"What church did you say you are from?"

"I didn't say. I'm from St. Paul's Church."

"I'm not familiar with it, but I do believe in God."

"Good. Well then, here are some materials…"

The man extended a small manila envelope out to Alex.

Instead of taking it, Alex put up a hand. "No. I really need to go. Sorry, and I don't mean to be rude."

A gentle click of the door put a wall of wooden silence between both of the men. A rude gesture, no doubt. He pulled back the curtain that covered the slender window next to the front door frame. The man cradling the unknown book sauntered down the sidewalk, yet passed several houses along his way until he climbed into a red sedan down the street.

"Dad, who was that?" Came David's voice from the hallway.

"Just a visitor, nothing to worry about."

Alex walked with David back to his bedroom, where the floor was covered in toys of all shapes and sizes. The walls of the room were painted a sky blue, and the wall opposite David's bed was covered with a beautiful mural of several biplanes weaving in between puffy, cotton-like clouds. On his son's dresser was another set of modern fighter jet models.

"How can you walk in here?" Alex said.

"What kind of visitor?"

"Somebody selling something or another, but I wasn't buying."

Alex then heard the kitchen phone ring and cringed. He hopscotched his way out of David's room and sprinted into the kitchen. The caller identification screen read "out of area". He waited for them to leave a message, but of course they did not.

He picked up the phone and dialed Todd Oliver. On the third ring, Todd answered.

"Hey, Todd. It's Alex. How are you?"

"Good, man. What's up?"

"You remember the conversation we had about the laptop?"

"Yep."

"Well, apparently things aren't over yet. I closed my account the other day at the bank and now I'm receiving all sorts of bizarre mail."

"That's weird."

"I don't mean to be a pest, but do you still have that laptop you found?"

"No."

"What did you do with it?"

"I did the tough thing. I turned it over."

For a moment Alex stood in silence.

"You okay?" Todd said.

"Sure. Thanks."

"Not a problem. Take care, man."

Alex said goodbye and hung up the phone. He ventured into the living room and found the family Bible on the coffee table. He opened it up to the Book of Isaiah, but then stopped a moment to pray. Nothing seemed to be making sense now, so he figured he would try a different tack.

"Lord, I don't understand. I did what you told me to do."

Alex opened his eyes and leafed through a few pages until the heading of chapter forty caught his eye. He read through the chapter, but verses 28-31 seemed to especially hold his attention:

> *Do you not know?*
> *Have you not heard?*
> *The Lord is the everlasting God,*
> *the Creator of the ends of the earth.*
>
> *He will not grow tired or weary,*
> *and his understanding no one can fathom.*

He gives strength to the weary
and increases the power of the weak.

Even youths grow tired and weary,
and young men stumble and fall;

but those who hope in the Lord
will renew their strength.

They will soar on wings like eagles;
they will run and not grow weary,
they will walk and not be faint.

He stood up and sighed, unsure of what the moment meant. He then walked over to the living room window and peered out from behind the curtains.

* * *

Kay left her aging tan Volvo in the parking lot and crunched her way towards a Payless shoe store in a strip mall near her home. A cold wind blew across the parking lot. The wind whipped up some snow that blew off a nearby snow bank and into her eyes. The snow hissed as it swept along the ground, and so she pressed her face under her teal scarf and stepped inside.

As she peeled back her scarf, she meandered over to the women's aisle. She read the shoe-size numbers off the black tags jutting out from the shelves. Upon finding the size-eight section, she scanned the open boxes for a pair of tan dress shoes. In minutes she found a potential perfect pair, but then a woman's raspy voice startled her.

Kay felt an immediate discomfort in her spirit as the woman spoke.

"Hi. Excuse me," the woman said. "Did I see you the other day at the rally on campus?"

Kay's turned around to see a woman dressed in a long, black wool coat with curly, reddish hair and piercing green eyes. The woman kept her hands in her pockets the entire time.

"Perhaps. Why?" Kay said.

"Good. I had a question for you."

Again, Kay felt an odd, hostile sensation near her heart, spreading throughout her body to her arms and down to her legs. She remained silent.

"Can you tell me more about your organization? I'm interested in helping with research. I've been doing some of my own and I'm a professor over at…"

"Listen, I'd love to talk, but I really need to get going." Kay glanced at her watch. "I'm sorry. It was nice to have met you."

Kay set the shoes back into their box and set the box back onto the aisle rack. She charged towards the door without looking back. She fumbled through her purse for her car keys. Instead she came across the wooden cross given to her at the campus rally. After another minute of frantic digging she scooped out her key ring in triumph.

As she opened her car door, she checked back towards the shoe store window to see the woman passing by the cash register and heading for the door. In seconds, Kay started her car, and with a lurch rolled out of her parking spot and sped off. Only then did the eerie feeling in her heart subside.

Chapter Thirty

The following Monday, James Malloy stepped out of the elevator on the tenth floor of the bank headquarters and entered through the glass double doors. On the way inside, he smiled and waved at Susan, who was at her desk looking at something on her monitor. She smiled politely in response, but said nothing.

He stopped at her desk and rested his elbows on top of the counter. To her left, he noticed a vase of fresh yellow roses. She did not seem to be wearing his favorite perfume anymore, however. "I'm curious," he said. "Is something going on around here?"

"I'm not sure what you mean, Mr. Malloy."

"Everybody's getting really rigid all of a sudden. Even you. And stop calling me Mr. Malloy. Call me Jim, like you used to."

"Nothing's going on, Mr. Malloy. Maybe it's the holidays."

"No, no. It's like…like…everybody's somber. Nice but somber. Like there's been a funeral."

Susan turned to look back towards her monitor. "Oh, wow," she said suddenly.

"What?"

"My sister sent me a picture. These bunnies are so cute."

"Bunnies," Malloy continued. "I'm talking about how somber everything is and you want to talk about bunnies. Say, nobody died did they?"

"I don't think so, Mr. Malloy."

"Hey, did you hear I'm giving out Christmas bonuses to everyone?"

"Really?"

He could see her eyes lit up again, like he had not seen in weeks. "Yeah, but everybody has to work a little harder. Mandatory sixty hour weeks for a month."

She scrunched her eyebrows and gave him a confused look.

172

"Ah, I'm just kiddin."

"That was a mean thing to say."

Malloy brushed her off and whistled to himself as he waltzed back to his office. The wall clock read four-thirty already and he could almost hear a brandy Coke calling his name. As he entered his office his desk phone rang.

"When are you coming home?" His wife said in a warm voice.

"Oh, soon. I said I'd meet somebody from down a couple floors at the bar. Then I'll head out."

He heard a loud sigh on the other end of the phone. Like usual, he rolled his eyes.

"I guess I won't see you 'til later. I've got choir practice tonight," his wife lamented.

"Ah. You and that new church thing. You know, maybe you should stop hanging out with that Kate woman. She's got your thinking all mixed up. She's a real piece of work."

"Goodbye, Jim."

"Yeah, bye."

He turned towards his computer monitor and began the shutdown process. He looked on one last time at the Seagle software on his desktop and smiled. The music file-sharing service was devious and brilliant all at once. He never used his version, however, because he knew that once you activated it via some music downloads, it would phone home at unpredictable intervals to a home server somewhere in Germany.

Or the Netherlands. Or Sweden. Or Japan.

He rubbed his hands together in anticipation because he knew that the administrators of the botnet would fire up the service again soon. In fact, he relished the thought of the network lighting up like a giant Christmas tree the day after Thanksgiving. A few weeks after that, more free account numbers and credit card data would roll in like Christmas presents delivered to his inbox.

* * *

An hour later Malloy pulled into the parking lot of a nearby Applebee's Restaurant. The lot was full because of the dinnertime crowd and as he made his way from the back part of the lot towards the front door, out of boredom he studied the customers leaving and entering the restaurant. He then noticed a lone figure in a dark jacket, standing underneath one of the restaurant's green, beige, and red awnings, as if he was waiting for a ride.

As Malloy approached, he realized the waiting customer was Charles Lantham. At first, he felt the instinct to look the other way, but he noticed Charles already spotted him.

"Hey," Charles said, bobbing his head.

"Hey Charles, how are you."

Charles stared at him briefly with glassy eyes and waved. He smelled of cheap vodka.

Malloy put his hands into his pockets and pulled out a business card. He extended it to Charles. "Say, uh, I heard about the little accident at work. If you need work, give me a call."

Charles slapped the card out of his hand. "I don't need your stinkin' job."

"Okay. See you around then."

"Whaddya mean accident?" Charles stammered.

Malloy turned away and ducked inside. He stood at the back of the line that waited for tables, hoping to move to the front instead. Out of the corner of his eye he saw Charles jabbing his finger at him, probably shouting expletives. He pretended not to notice, as if the window glass separated himself from a zoo exhibit.

He noticed an orange and black taxi pulling up a moment later. Charles continued to spout off despite the taxi driver getting out of his vehicle in an attempt to draw his attention. The hostess meanwhile offered to take down Malloy's name, but he refused and passed onwards towards the bar.

"Do you know that man?" She said, referring to Charles, who now had one foot in the taxi and another on the curb. Charles continued to shout something or another, but the sound was garbled at best through the window.

"Who? Him? Can't say I do," Malloy said with a chuckle.

* * *

Later in the evening, Alex sat on the sofa with his wife, planning out their budget on Alex's laptop. Several piles of old bills were spread out across the sofa and the coffee table. Alex sat hunched over his laptop when he received a new e-mail. It was from the generic Yahoo! e-mail address and addressed to everyone on the LAMPS mailing list.

> All,
>
> We have just found out we are being tracked. We're not sure who is behind it (yet) but we have some idea. If you attended the rally, you may be a target. We've also found out that someone was handing out crosses at the rally. The cross may have a tracking device embedded inside of it. If you have one of these, disable it and let us know.
>
> Brian
>
> P.S. We're using a temporary address because our main site is offline. It's been under a massive DDOS attack for hours.

Alex looked up from his screen and stared at Danielle.

She stared back without blinking, and widened her eyes while smiling. "Now what?"

"Go downstairs and grab the smallest saw I have. Some sandpaper, too."

"Why?"

"Trust me."

"That's not a good thing to say after you just got done staring somebody down."

"Please. Just get me a saw."

"You're staring at me and you want me to trust with a saw?"

"Please."

"Fine."

She stood up and went downstairs. Minutes later Danielle returned with a keyhole saw and a sheet of coarse sandpaper.

Alex took the items from her and set them on the coffee table. "Oh, and get me the garbage can."

"Budgets make you cranky, you know that? Bossy, too."

Danielle finally obliged and handed him the wastebasket from the kitchen.

Alex stood up and went into the bedroom. He dug around in his desk drawer and found the wooden cross he received at the rally. Clutching it with his hand, he returned to the living room and set it down on the edge of the table on top. He then put the wastebasket on the carpet beneath that.

With a few quick strokes of the saw, he sliced it in half, and then cradled both halves in his hands.

Danielle put her hands to her mouth. "Oh my…"

Alex put up a hand.

Her eyes then widened. "What on earth do you think you're doing, Mr. Poole?"

"Trust me."

"I don't."

"Look," Alex said, practically scolding her.

Inside one half of the wood, he noticed something hard, black and glasslike. After several scuffs of sandpaper, he revealed a tiny glass capsule with tiny electronics inside. He held it up between his thumb and forefinger to show her.

"Where is David, by the way?" He asked suddenly.

"In his room playing. Why?"

"Danielle, I think you should switch banks as soon as possible."

"Ya think?"

The telephone rang a few seconds later. Alex grabbed the crème-colored cordless phone off the couch and answered.

"Hey Alex, it's Ian."

"Ian, buddy. What's up?"

"I've got something for you. Remember when we talked about the laptops ending up all over the place? I had a friend tip me off about where some of the accounts might have come from. Seems he's been poking around on some carders forums lately."

"And?"

"Some of the data came from The Flock."

"The Flock?"

"It's a 100,000 machine botnet that was built using some music file-sharing software. I think the front end software's called Seagle. People trade songs and play lists online with it. Anyway, some of the music programs randomly phone home and some malware gets sent back. Then the software sucks up any account info on their system using key loggers. You don't have any of that installed right?"

"I better check." Suddenly, Alex felt as if he had been socked in the stomach by a boxer.

"If you know anybody that has it, have them drop it like a bad habit. Hey, you don't think your friend at the bank had anything to with that do you?"

"Good question. I wouldn't doubt it. It's getting weird here, though, Ian. I'm getting weird junk mail, and I just found a tracking device. I'm also had a strange guy come up to my door. Oh and hey, remember that guy that hit my account?"

"Yeah?"

"I found 'em."

"Awesome."

Alex went into the den and fired up the computer. In a couple of minutes, his desktop came up onscreen. There, in the middle of the screen was an icon for Seagle, with its black, white, and sky blue seagull logo.

"Hey, Ian? Bad news. I found it. Haven't used it in a long time, though," Alex said.

"Uninstall it, pronto. I'll shoot you an e-mail with a list of other files you'll have to take out."

Alex's shoulders sagged as he uninstalled the software and wrote some notes down for future reference. "I wonder how it got my data, though," he thought out loud. Then, he spotted a tax software icon and thought about some other budgeting software he had used one time.

"So, wait. I don't understand," Alex said. "Tell me more about the botnet."

"The Flock? Yeah, it's got a lot of capabilities. It can be used to launch DDoS attacks, track users, launch mass amounts of spam, you name it. It's quite the weapon. And it can rented for a price, I hear."

Alex sighed and looked at the tracking device which he still clutched in his left hand. "I think I get it now."

"You know who's behind the botnet?"

"No, but I get it. You called the thing The Flock. The music software is called Seagle. Flock of Seagles. Get it?"

There was a pause on the other end of the line that lasted a good fifteen seconds. "And here I thought my stories were bad," Ian said.

Alex returned to the living room to see his wife sorting through some bills.

"Hey you want to hear a story?" Ian said after a moment.

Alex looked on at his laptop and the budget spreadsheet. "Maybe another time. I'm working on something with the wife."

"Gotcha. Take care."

Alex hung up the phone and went downstairs to smash the tracking device with a hammer.

Chapter Thirty-One

Nearly two weeks later, Kay sat in the dark next to Brian, waiting inside of Brian's dark blue rusty Escort. A few blocks down she could see a shadowy figure moving back and forth from a vehicle to the side door of a long, two-story warehouse. She watched the figure peel back a tarp that was covering a trailer and then lift up a box and set it onto the ground. The figure pulled out three more boxes and then stood still as if to take a breath.

"No, you were right, Brian. That's Ben alright," she said.

She handed him the binoculars and sighed.

Brian picked up a towel by his feet and wiped off the accumulating fog from the driver's side window. "It looks like he's using a dolly of some sort. Moving some crates in or something," he said, looking through the binoculars.

"Think we should move in?"

"Naw. Let him go. When he takes off we'll pull up."

Kay took the binoculars back and waited. Ten more minutes passed before Ben brought the dolly back and loaded it onto his car trailer. He then pulled the tarp over the trailer, locked up the warehouse door, and pulled away down the alley.

"He sure picked a bad night," Brian said after a moment.

"Why?"

"Full moon's out. Snow's on the ground. If I only had a camera on me. Or my night vision goggles."

After waiting another two minutes Brian started his car. A ting-ting-ting sound came from the engine as it ran, echoing down the alley and triggering a barking dog somewhere. He crept along the backside of the warehouse, and as they neared the delivery door, Brian stopped the car and killed the engine.

Kay jumped out first with a flashlight and ran up to the door. She ran her hand along its surface, feeling several rust spots and dents.

She then pointed out the lock to Brian.

Brian followed a moment later with a bolt cutter and a crowbar in hand. Upon reaching the door, he waved her back. He then proceeded to shear off the lock with the bolt cutter.

Kay opened the warehouse door and flicked on her flashlight. Her breath created clouds of mist in the cold, dank darkness of the warehouse. She went ahead of Brian and swung the flashlight around making wide arcs first along the floor, and then a few feet above the ground. Dusty moonbeams struck the ground through various windows, but it was not enough to help discern the way forward.

For a moment, she stood motionless, anticipating a person, a mouse, or some kind of movement inside. When she heard nothing, she slipped forward, scanning the ground before her, until her eyes fell on a series of tarps in the far corner.

"Let's be extra careful in here. I smell a little bit of gasoline in the air," Brian said, taking the flashlight from her. "Whatever we do, we have to keep the light on. No creating sparks."

He crept ahead, steadily approaching several dark blue tarps and one black one. Then he reached out to one of them and lifted it up. "Here, hold the flashlight a minute."

With the beam directed at one of the crates, Brian slung back the tarp, and revealed numerous crates of similar shape and size. Crowbar in hand, he began to pry at the top of one of them. For a second, he glanced back at the alley door. Some of the nails sprang loose with a creak, and inside were a dozen or so empty glass bottles of various shapes and sizes.

"What do you make of it?" Kay asked.

"Let's open another."

"Maybe we should close up this one first, though."

Brian slammed his fist onto the top of the opened crate, but did a poor job of securing it back into place. He rapped it a few times with his crowbar, cringing at the noise it made. "Oh, never mind. Let's check on another. Here, shine the light under that tarp to the left."

Brian readjusted the tarp back into place, and lifted another. Again, he pried open another crate, although not as far, and this time found more empty glass bottles. He pushed that top back into place and directed her to a black tarp that seemed to be set off apart from the rest. He held up the tarp with one hand, while Kay swept over its mysteries with the flashlight.

Here were brown drums, not crates, with the lids sealed shut. A clear, plastic hose lay coiled up on top of the first drum she looked at. Brian unscrewed the rusted metal cap on top of one of the drums. Within seconds, they were both struck with the suffocating odor of gasoline. He quickly retightened the cap.

"Looks like a firebomb factory to me, Kay," he said with a sigh.

"I think we should get out of here."

"I agree."

Kay kept the flashlight aimed at the floor as they snuck back up to the exit door. Near the door, she saw a blue tarp covering up a smaller object. She pointed the flashlight at it and peeled the tarp back. "Hand me the crowbar," she said in a commanding voice.

She popped the top off of the top crate and peered inside. "What do you make of this?"

Brian looked inside. "Weird."

He reached into the crate and pulled out an object that looked like some kind of shoulder-fired launcher. "It looks like a homemade launcher of some sort." He threw the device back into the crate.

"Whoa," Kay said after a moment. She banged the top of the crate shut with the crowbar. In the distance, she heard voices that seemed to be coming from around one of the walls of the warehouse. Kay opened the door, and peered out into the moonlit, snow-covered alley. Then she doused the flashlight. She peered up and down the alley, but noticed nothing unusual. Brian let the delivery door shut with a subtle click.

"Brian, I'm concerned about this," Kay whispered.

"You know, I thought it was a great turnout at the rally, until I realized I didn't recognize a lot of the crowd at all. Makes you wonder who some of those people really were."

"What about the lock?"

Brian grimaced. He walked around to the hatchback of his car and opened it up. He dug around inside for something and then pulled out a small propane torch. He held it up to Kay, whose eyes widened. "Get in the car. I'll hurry."

She watched him slip on a pair of protective glasses and turn a knob on the torch. He squeezed his spark lighter and lit the torch. He then proceeded to weld the delivery door shut around where the handle portion of the door met the strike plate. She watched as the blue flame hissed and heated the door, creating a cloud of steam in the cold night air.

He then turned off his torch and ran towards the car.

Just as he opened his car door, Kay heard a male voice coming from somewhere down the alley. "Hey, Brian, how are you. Great speech the other day."

"Thanks," Brian muttered, climbing into the driver's seat.

"What's with the crowbar, Brian?"

"C'mon, Brian, keep moving," Kay said, tugging at his coat. She noticed three figures now walking towards the car. "Hurry up, start the car."

Brian then rolled down his window. "What are you doing in that warehouse? I hope you're not planning on setting off a bunch of firebombs."

One of the figures laughed. It looked like another male. "What are you talking about?"

"There were crates of bottles in there. And gasoline."

"Why don't you two just run along home now," the same figure said.

"Roll up your window!" Kay yelled.

"What makes you think we're in danger?" Brian said without concern.

Brian looked ahead and attempted to start his car. Only after several turns of the engine did it finally start. He slammed his car into reverse and rolled down the alley until they backed into a cross street. Before the figures could catch up to them, Brian slammed his car into drive and sped off.

Chapter Thirty-Two

Several days later, Alex and Danielle drove home from dinner at her brother's house by taking several back streets. It was a cool, clear night and the traffic remained light despite the approaching holiday. Along the way, they passed by several homes with extensive Christmas light displays and Nativity scenes. At one point, Alex half-wondered if some of the displays could be seen from outer space.

The roads and sidewalks were free of snow tonight. As Alex drove on, he noticed a man walking along the shoulder of the road, but stumbling every twenty feet or so.

"Guy's drunk over there," he said.

"Be careful."

"I am."

Alex gave the man extra room to walk as he passed by and continued on towards a stop sign. A thought came into his mind: *Help that man.*

Alex groaned and tightened his grip on the steering wheel as he came to a stop. He sat at the stop sign for a minute and looked back at the figure in the dark via his rearview mirror. The man continued to stumble.

"What's wrong?" Danielle asked.

"I'm supposed to help that guy," he said, purposely mumbling his words.

He pulled ahead through the intersection and pulled into the next driveway he found.

"Didn't you just shampoo the upholstery in here?" Danielle said.

"So?"

"So, what if he stinks the car up?"

Alex frowned. "Well, lemme just pass him by again and go from there."

"I'd hate to have him throw up in the back seat. And you won't be using *our* carpet cleaner to vacuum that out."

Alex rolled his eyes. He passed by the man again, and this time from the front side. In an instant he recognized him. "Wow. That was Charles. My ex-coworker."

"No."

"Still want me to keep on driving?"

Danielle was silent.

Alex drove on another couple of blocks and then pulled into another driveway to turn around. He then slowed down as he approached his former co-worker again. He pulled up a few car lengths in front of him and parked the car.

Danielle crossed her arms. "I thought you didn't like him."

Alex got out of his car and ran around the back of it to meet up with Charles. "Hey. Charles. It's me, Alex."

Charles stopped and shivered, with his hands in his jacket pockets. "Oh, hey Alex." He dug around for something in his pocket. "Hey man. I gots sometheen for you. Where'd it go? Oh yeah...here."

Charles pulled out something metallic and placed it in Alex's hand.

Alex looked down at the object. "It's a bottle cap."

"No man. Oh man."

"Here, let me give you a ride home."

Charles put up a hand as if to reassure Alex. "No, man. I got it."

"Not really. You're stumbling."

"I'm not stumblin'." At that Charles tripped on something or another, but regained his balance.

Alex put an arm around Charles' shoulder and led him up to the car. He opened the back door and watched as Charles climbed into the car in slow motion. A few seconds later, Charles laid down across the back seat, facing up. By now Alex could see Danielle rolling down her window a crack.

"Do you know where to take him?" Danielle asked.

"His house is about two miles up the road here."

"Two miles?"

Alex shut the back door and climbed back into the driver's seat. He heard his friend groan a few times and then fall silent. The smell of alcohol caused him to roll down his window a bit and turn up the heater.

Alex drove on in silence and eventually pulled into Charles' driveway. He parked the car, got out, and opened the back door. As if on cue, Charles blinked his eyes and woke up.

"I wuzzent sleeping," Charles said.

"Time to go home, Charles. We're here."

Alex watched as Charles sat up and slowly worked his way to the door. Foot by foot, Alex helped the once proud sales guy out of the car and up the front steps. "Is your wife home?"

"Sheesh. No. We're sepa…sepa…I can't talk tonight. Separated."

Charles' house was a two-story, two-garage, pale-blue-and-white place at the end of a cul-de-sac. The yard was well kept, although Alex noticed the house seemed unusually dark inside.

Alex heard Charles mumble something incoherent and watched him fumble with his house keys. Alex took the house keys from him and let him inside. He held the front door open as Charles gravitated towards the bedroom. The interior contained hardwood floors, a few stunning impressionistic paintings on the living room walls and earth tones for wall colors. Several crushed beer cans were scattered around on top of the coffee table in the living room, however.

He trailed Charles into the bedroom and flipped on the light. Charles gingerly slipped off his shoes and collapsed on the bed. On the walls were Minnesota Wild posters and a picture of geese flying over a lake in the fall. On his dresser were trophies from high school, now collecting dust.

At that, Alex turned off the light and left the room.

"Why you helping me man?" Charles said as Alex entered the living room.

"It's a long story. Get some sleep and call me sometime. We'll talk."

Alex left via the front door and returned to his car. He started the engine but laughed as Danielle waved a newspaper in an effort to clear the air.

∗ ∗ ∗

An hour later, Ben snuck out of his car. He planned on unloading one more crate of glass bottles at the warehouse, but this time they were stashed in the front seat of his car. He knew his recent trips to the warehouse with the trailer were starting to draw the attention of a neighbor or two when he spotted a police cruiser circling the block a few times the other night.

He walked up to the delivery door of the warehouse and noticed his lock lying on the ground. Then he saw the crude weld between the door and the door frame. In vain, he tried to pull on the handle several times. He pulled his hand through his hair and kicked the door.

He looked up to see if any windows were reachable with a ladder. The windows all appeared to be several feet over his head and too small to bother with smashing them in anyway. With one kick, he punted the sheared lock down the alley and dashed back to his car.

* * *

Within an hour, Ben crossed the St. Croix River and the Minnesota-Wisconsin state line on Interstate 94. On the floor of his car, underneath a yellow blanket, sat the wooden crate packed with several empty wine bottles and a paper bag full of cheap plastic cigarette lighters. He glanced at the road map on the passenger seat with a flashlight with one hand still on the steering wheel. It was at least a four-hour drive to the Walworth county jail in Wisconsin. By his own calculations there was still time to meet his father, and maybe even free him, for in two days his father was to be transferred to a state correctional facility in Racine.

His hunger got the best of him, though, and by the time he reached Lake Delton near the Wisconsin Dells, he decided to pull off of the interstate and parked at a nearby Denny's restaurant. Suddenly, the lights on his dashboard began to dim and brighten erratically. He swore. He slapped the dash with the palm of his hand but it had no effect.

Upon pulling into the restaurant parking lot, he noticed the smell of oil coming from his engine. He parked and opened up the hood. A few splotches of oil were splattered on the underside of the hood and on the sides of the engine. He swore again. Then he slammed the hood shut and entered the restaurant.

Once inside, he seated himself at a booth and waited for the waitress. The bar rush crowd had yet to materialize, although there appeared to be a steady stream of travelers and truck drivers coming off of the nearby interstate.

Minutes passed. The waitress stopped by with a glass of ice water and a menu, but out of the corner of his eye, Ben noticed a strange flicker of light. He turned around in his seat to see a police officer shining his flashlight around his car and into the windows. Ben glanced away when the second the officer looked over at him.

He waited for the officers to leave. The one with the flashlight did not, and he noticed yet another officer climbing out of the patrol car and then entering the restaurant. That officer looked in his direction.

The waitress returned a minute later.

"I'm ready," Ben said, without opening the menu.

"Ready sweetie?"

He smiled. "I'll take a Grand Slam."

"Awright. You sure are out kinda late, hon. Everything alright?"

"Just fine, ma'am."

She took the menu from him and left the table. Not even a second passed and one of the officers entered the restaurant. Soon he approached Ben's table. A husky, menacing voice caught Ben by surprise.

"Sir, are you the owner of that car out there?" The officer said.

Ben flinched. "I am."

"Could I see your driver's license?"

Ben reached into his back pocket, withdrew his wallet, and handed over his license. He watched closely as the officer held it in his hand a minute. By now the waitress had slipped into the kitchen.

"Sir, I need you to step outside with me for a moment," the officer commanded.

Ben wanted the officer to lead the way, but the officer directed Ben out the door first instead. He directed Ben over towards the car and then turned on his own flashlight. The other officer took Ben's license and sat inside the squad car.

"It smells like you have an oil leak here. Have you taken this into the shop yet?" The officer asked.

"No, sir."

Ben watched as the officers exchanged glances. The officer in the police cruiser glanced up and shook his head up and down after checking on the license.

"Are you aware this vehicle has expired tabs?" The officer growled.

"I just hadn't gotten around to gettin' 'em yet."

"I assume you also know you are driving with a revoked license, correct?"

Silence.

"Would you mind opening up the passenger door?"

Ben obliged and stepped back, calculating the location of each officer, the location of the bushes around him, and the shortest path away from the situation. The officer did not look to be in the best of shape, Ben reasoned.

He opened up the door and stood back. The officer then pulled back the yellow blanket covering the crate and the bag full of lighters. At this point Ben turned to run.

"Hey!" The officer yelled.

Ben jumped over a row of bushes and ran into a nearby field. He thrashed through several patches of dead weeds. Footsteps pounded the hardened earth behind him. In seconds, he found a dirt road and picked up some speed.

One hundred feet later his foot caught a rock, sending him tumbling into a culvert and then into the half-frozen muck of a marsh. A cattail jabbed him in the leg. He wiped some mud off his face, and tried to stand up. In a blur of pain and shadows, he gasped for air as an officer tackled him from behind.

* * *

Early the next morning, James Malloy backed out of his driveway to head out for work. The light of dawn began to overtake the sky now, shifting it from a deep blue to a peach color in a matter of minutes. His silver BMW glided down a side street and on towards the highway as if it were a cloud riding the jet stream. Since it was near the top of the hour, he decided to flip on the radio and listen to the news.

"Several area banks are being investigated due the spate of mass identity thefts over the past several months..."

That was more than he wanted to hear. He already had been notified by a trembling subordinate of two pending investigations by the feds. *How was it his fault*, he wondered, *that his competitors did not always maintain a high level of security with their customer information? How was it his fault he leveraged the system to his own benefit?*

Wasn't that what business was all about anyway?

He grabbed what he thought was an Elvis disc from his collection on his car's sun visor and jammed the disc into his car's player. Seconds later, he heard the opening lines of the song *Renegade* coming from his speakers.

Chapter Thirty-Three

In the dream, Alex watched as a small unmarked frigate lurched and heaved on the ocean. The lights onboard were dark and no one appeared to be on deck. Seconds later, a missile flew out of the deck of the frigate, shearing its way through a bank of dense fog. A bright, white-hot streak of cloud and flame arced into the sky with a roar. As the roar faded, shouts of joy erupted in an unfamiliar language.

Seconds later, in an office of a financial services company, a sales representative stood up from his cubicle to stretch. He picked up his red-and-white Boston Red Sox coffee cup and wandered over to the window to watch the fierce blizzard now enshrouding the city. The visibility dropped to the point where one could only see across the company parking lot to the neighboring three-story business building, and the cars in the lot became caked in white. The dark brown light poles in the lot rocked in the wind and in the distance the flow of traffic on a nearby freeway seized up.

Then, the power went out.

A collective gasp could be heard across the floor, as well as groans from various corners of the department, as they were plunged into darkness. The man turned back towards his terminal, but suddenly his cup dropped to the floor. Coffee splashed across the carpet with a popping sound as he clutched the back of his hand in apparent agony.

The man turned over his hand and a bubbling, blackened patch of skin appeared where his access chip had been. Screams echoed across the floor, from cubicle to cubicle. A blond-haired woman in her twenties lunged towards him with a tiny orange flame jet shooting out from the back of her right hand.

At that, Alex woke up to find himself wrapped up in his blanket. He looked over at his alarm clock and grimaced. It was ten in the morning.

Groggy, he stood up and headed into the living room. The house remained shrouded in silence. There was plenty of light in the living room for Danielle appeared to have opened all the curtains earlier that morning. The bright sunlight hurt his eyes, however.

He wandered over to the coffee table to find the remote control. The coffee table remained covered in resumes, classified ads, and paperwork from his job hunt the night before. With one blast of the remote, the television screen exploded to life.

"...investigations are continuing this morning in the recent identity theft crisis that has struck several local banks including CamdenBank. Investigators are also looking to see if there any connections between the disappearance of numerous laptops with financial information and executives at Aspirizon Bank. Already this morning lines are forming outside a couple of the banks as angry customers are withdrawing their money. In other news..."

He smirked at the report and then wandered into the dining room. A bundle of mail sat on the table from the night before that included more beer paraphernalia. His digital camera sat nearby on top of a bookcase, in anticipation of more strange visitors at his door. This time, he figured, he wanted to be ready.

He paused a moment and stared out the window at the crisp December day that was unfolding. A rabbit bounded away from the house through the snow towards a far fence. He then turned to go into the kitchen and gazed upon his still-unfinished jigsaw puzzle on the card table.

It looked as if Danielle or David had dropped in more pieces over the past week because the pile of unplaced pieces was smaller. Also, more of the outer portions of the puzzle had been filled in to reveal more sky, ocean, rocks and ocean spray. After that, he glanced over at the calendar on the kitchen wall.

It was day forty.

His eyes shot over to the clock on the wall. In an instant, he ran back into his bedroom.

He lunged into the closet and grabbed the nearest sweatshirt. A pair of blue jeans later, he found himself back in the kitchen, double-checking the calendar as he combed his hair.

He slipped on a pair of sneakers and scooped up his jacket from the hallway closet. After all, if Aspirizon Bank was indeed going to be overthrown, then he wanted a front row seat at the headquarters if possible.

He dashed downstairs, but when he reached the service door to the garage, he stopped, dropped his head, and immediately went into a brief prayer for guidance. He reflected a moment to think that maybe what he was doing was selfish or that maybe Malloy at some point took the message to heart and changed his ways.

Then he thought about the last few weeks.

He hit the garage door button, and jumped into his car. From the glove compartment, he pulled out a roadmap. There were multiple locations worth investigating, from Lindemeier Consulting to the Aspirizon Bank's main headquarters in Bloomington. The best action, he decided, would probably be at the headquarters itself. He buckled himself in and steeled himself for whatever would come next.

* * *

By eleven-thirty in the morning, Alex was over halfway to the bank. What should have been a half hour drive turned into an hour long ordeal because of an accident near the Minneapolis St. Paul International Airport. Traffic crept along at ten miles per hour or less at times, leaving Alex to wonder if God was trying to block his path or at least get him to reconsider.

Eventually, he came upon the accident scene which involved a white truck full of turkeys which flipped over onto its side. There were police cars everywhere with their lights flashing. Somehow, a few turkeys apparently had escaped and they were now running around in one of the ditches alongside the highway.

As soon as he passed the accident scene, his cell phone rang. He glanced at the screen and noticed it was Danielle. "Good morning, Mrs. Poole."

"Mrs. Poole? Where are you by the way? I tried calling home because I thought you'd still be in bed."

"I'm en route to Bloomington. I should be there in about ten minutes. How did the dentist appointment go?"

"Fine. Bloomington? Have you been listening to the news?"

"You bet. There are turkeys everywhere. They must be freezing out here."

"Ugh, no. Did you hear about the bank? Did you hear about the crowds gathering? Wait…you're not heading into that are you?"

Alex remained silent and smiled.

"Alex, what are you doing?"

"Oh nothing."

Alex could hear David in the background asking what was going on.

"Well, I'm pulling into David's school now and dropping him off," Danielle said. "I think you should go back home."

"Why? I'll be okay. Trust me on this. I don't know how it's going to unfold, but God is watching over me."

The other end of the phone seemed to fall silent.

"Danielle? You still there?"

She then dropped her voice to a whisper. "Alex, they were talking on the radio about protesters with picket signs. The police are on their way."

"Front row seats, here I come. Listen, my battery is starting to go out on my phone. I'll call you as soon as I get down there and know more about the situation."

"Alex…"

"Know what? I've never seen a bank overthrown before…"

The battery went dead on his phone. In frustration, he whipped it into the backseat of his car. His knuckles began to pale as he gripped the steering wheel tighter. Sighing, he scanned the side roads along the interstate for signs of trouble. The traffic flowed smooth and swift now like a river current into Bloomington.

Beads of sweat laced his palms as his hands clutched the tacky steering wheel. In spite of the speech he gave Danielle, his insides were churning. He hoped the radio reports proved to be mere hype. He breathed deep again and straightened up in his seat, eyes darting around him as he exited the freeway.

* * *

A few blocks from the bank headquarters he saw a city patrol car heading towards the bank, sirens off but lights flashing. He decided to park on a side street for the time being. After all, what was the use of getting into yet another traffic jam near the building? The radio reports were of little help now in terms of gauging how big the crowd really was and if any of the protests had turned violent.

He bounded out of his car and monitored the sidewalks around him. Up ahead on the sidewalk he could see some people walking towards the general direction of the headquarters building which stood some ten stories high in the distance. The glass windows of the building took on an almost eerie glow now in the hazy noontime sun.

His breathing intensified. Inside, he felt as if there were several electric currents circuiting his body, increasing in strength with every step. As he arrived at the parking lot, he saw a group of at least twenty rowdy protesters on the sidewalk in front of the building. A short line of customers extended outside the door and some even interacted with the protesters, who were handing out brochures and jabbing picket signs in the air. He noticed more cars lining up along the street as the parking lot filled and so he, too, decided to stand in line.

Within minutes, the line surged forward. Alex realized the crowd was becoming impatient in their efforts to occupy as much space as they could in the lobby. The crowd of protesters, however, seemed unfamiliar to him. As the line in the lobby moved towards the door, one of the protesters singled him out and tapped him forcefully on the shoulder.

"Hey, sir. Do you know where you're money is?" A man asked him. The man looked to be barely in his twenties, with long, pony-tailed brown hair, a goatee, and intense eyes.

"It's not here," Alex said with a slight grin.

"Good for you!" The man shouted. "Here, take one of these."

Alex grabbed the material the man handed him, but found it was a LAMPS brochure. Alex tried his best to place anybody's face within the group of protesters but he could not recognize any of them.

He soon found himself in the bank lobby. Out of the corner of his eye, he spotted a television station camera crew setting up in the corner. They engaged themselves in a conversation with a nearby security guard. To the left, the lounge furniture was filled with customers, some standing, some sitting, but all waiting. To the right, the familiar curved teller counter with its black, smooth, flowing marble looked like a breakwater against the tide of people.

How he wanted to just sit or stand in the corner and watch Malloy deal with this mess. Yet one of the arguing customers and a helpless teller soon grabbed his attention. It looked like the same teller who helped his close his account at CamdenBank. Her teller window nameplate even read "Robin". He watched her reactions a moment. He noticed her wipe a tear from her eye as a man in his late fifties yelled and gestured wildly with his hands.

A sense of conviction washed over Alex. He plunged ahead through the crowd and found the elevators again at the end of a short, carpeted hallway. Despite some complaints overheard along the way, he entered an open car and jabbed at the tenth floor button. His heart began to race. He paced back and forth inside the rising elevator, thinking of his next move.

In seconds, the elevator doors popped open. At one end of the black-tiled hallway he saw the double glass doors again, and Susan behind the reception desk. He paced up to the doors and grabbed the door handle. With one pull, he darted inside.

Susan was in the middle of arguing with a caller when he arrived. Today she wore a blue and white flower-print dress, with pony-tailed hair and large, silver hoop earrings. After a moment of heated debate, she slammed down the phone and sighed loudly.

Alex put his hands onto the reception desk and burst into a speech. "I need to see Mr. Malloy. Now, please."

At first, she did not seem to even notice that he was there. Then: "You're brave, you know that?" She looked off towards the hallway that led to Malloy's office and then back at Alex. "You didn't find another car did you?"

"No."

"Okay. Was he expecting you?"

"Yes and no." Alex drummed his fingers on the desktop. "I mean, it's urgent."

"You'll have to take a seat over there."

"Listen, I can't sit down and wait. You have a mob in your lobby that's growing by the minute." He patted the cherrywood-topped desk a moment and watched as her features turned from unconcern to sudden puzzlement.

She picked up the telephone again and dialed Malloy's office. Seconds passed. Then: "Odd. He's not answering."

Susan grew suddenly pale. "Let me call the front security desk."

"Turn on a radio."

"I'm sorry?"

"Here, hand that little radio on your desk to me." Before she could even turn to look at it, he snatched the small, black-and-silver radio off of her desk. He changed to the AM radio band and tuned in a news station. Word was the crowds were now beginning to spread to other Aspirizon Bank branches. In the distance, Alex heard police sirens. "Believe me now?"

"I'll call him again. Wait a minute. Mr. Malloy should be out here soon. He has an interview downstairs with Channel Nine at twelve-thirty."

As Alex set the radio back down on her desk, Malloy emerged from the hallway off to the right of the welcome desk.

Susan stood up. "Mr. Malloy, Alex is here to see you."

Malloy glared at Alex in a way that he had not seen in years.

"I know," said Alex, putting his hands out as if to plead with Malloy. "I have a lotta nerve for coming back here. But you have a mob downstairs. I suggest you go down there and to calm them down before they tear this place apart."

"What mob?"

"Look out your windows at your parking lot. Better yet, follow me." Alex charged back out through the double doors, half-expecting Malloy to ignore him. Instead, he found the bank president right behind him.

Alex stepped into an open elevator car and glanced towards the ceiling, then back at Malloy. "Jim, this may be your last chance."

"My last chance for what?"

"Peace."

"So you're the one doing all this."

"I had nothing to do with this."

"Riiight. Or is it God's fault?"

As the doors closed, a sudden unease came over Alex. He glanced over at the digital readout near the elevator door.

Malloy stood there with his hands in his pockets. "You're a real piece of work these days I tell you. Level with me. Did you get caught up with LAMPS?"

Alex stared at the floor then back at Malloy. "No. Now level with me. Do you like flooding mailboxes with junk? Did you send your minions out to spy on my family?"

Malloy became visibly agitated. "Did you ever steal software from me?"

"Not on your life. Did you ever load up a bunch of laptops with stolen information picked up by a botnet and then get a bunch of petty thieves and addicts to do your dirty work for ya?"

Malloy gave him a snide look that might normally work on his employees, but did not faze Alex. "What are you babbling about?"

"How's the chip business these days, Jim?"

Malloy smashed his thumb on the red stop button on the elevator but it refused to function. He hit other floor buttons, and although they lit up, the elevator car continued to drop. He swore and pounded his fist on the wall. "Why isn't this thing working?"

He opened up a small metal panel on the wall of the elevator and picked up the black telephone inside. The line, however, remained dead. He swore again and slammed the receiver back on the hook. He then shoved a finger into Alex's chest and snarled. "What do you want from me? What's your game this time, Poole?"

"Do you ever get that *sinking feeling*, Jim?"

As the elevator bottomed out at street level, they could both hear the chanting of the crowd outside as well as much yelling. Alex dreaded the thought of a stampede. The doors popped open before them.

Malloy gave Alex an incredulous look. He stepped into the hallway towards the lobby and shouted over towards the security desk, which was already overrun. The crowd seem to stretch out in all directions, filling in the lobby area like high tide, increasing in number and obscuring the view of the parking lot.

Alex felt a sudden strong push in his spirit, and turned to fire a steely glance at the crowd. He then turned to face Malloy, putting himself between him and the crowd which began to surge forward again. As the crowd pushed in to close in on the both of them, Malloy somehow found his way towards the teller desk.

"Everybody, can I have your attention," he shouted. "I'm sure the events of the last day or so have you upset. Rest assured your money is safe here. We're doing…"

Several members of the crowd began to yell again. One man yelled out, "Not with a fink like you running the show! I want my money."

Malloy fired a nasty look back at Alex. "And you'll have your money. We're investigating this internally."

"But you're the fraud!" A woman shouted.

Malloy stood motionless as the customers began yelling at him again. Alex could see the color draining from his features. Malloy then went behind the teller line and said something to one of his employees. Alex could see the security guard finally heading over towards Malloy, for what it was worth. He could also see a handful of officers making their way through the rear entrance of the bank.

"Go home," Malloy yelled back to the crowd.

"What?" A customer shouted from the back.

"Go home," Malloy said, a bit louder.

Alex could see the picket signs bobbing up and down outside, along with fists being pumped up into the air. A crowd was even gathering outside the windows, pressing their noses up to the glass. He heard more sirens and could see the crowd near the front doors parting as if somebody important was coming through.

Two police officers then pushed their way through the crowd in the lobby as the television news crew stood by filming every minute. Alex could see Malloy backing away from the teller desk and making a break for his office. Several customers blocked his path, however.

One of the officers shouted. "Mr. Malloy! Mr. Malloy!"

In seconds, Malloy was cornered.

"We have a warrant for your arrest," the officer yelled.

Malloy attempted to put as many customers between himself and the cops as he could, but several customers cleared a path this time. One officer took the president by his shoulders and put his hands behind his back. The handcuffs followed as a murmur swept through the crowd.

Then Alex heard a shout from behind him. It was Danielle.

She pushed her way through the revolving doors in back and ran up to embrace him.

He kissed her flush on the lips. "What are you doing here?"

"This place is surrounded by cops."

"I know."

"C'mon, let's go." She tugged at his hand and he readily gave in.

They pushed their way towards the back doors. "You're right. I can't do anything here." They hurried out past the elevators and through the revolving doors, not wanting to turn back.

Outside the sky began to cloud over, but there was no wind. They headed towards their cars. In minutes, Alex saw Malloy being escorted outside to a waiting squad car. It was then that he noticed a group of Christmas carolers walking up the street, singing hymns and Christmas songs.

"Isn't that Jim's wife?" Alex said to Danielle, studying the faces of the singers.

"Where?"

"Over there. In the choir."

The group kept walking right along in front of the bank, singing, "Angels We Have Heard On High."

Alex turned to look back at Malloy as he was being helped into the police car. He appeared to be swearing, yet shaken. Alex could see him staring at the carolers as they passed by. In that moment, Alex could also see in Malloy's eyes a look of both dread and shock. If it really was Malloy's wife in the choir, he thought, then her voice was nothing short of beautiful. Oddly enough, it even seemed to make her sing even more boldly.

Chapter Thirty-Four

The day before Christmas Eve, Alex and Danielle finished up the last of their Christmas shopping at Ridgedale Mall. The sky was remarkably crisp, clear, and blue in a way that only a winter day could bring. The ground was covered in a thin, fresh blanket of fluffy snow from the night before that looked a bit like flaked coconut. As for the parking lot around the mall, it was filled to the hilt with cars, trucks, and the sounds of Salvation Army bell ringers in front of certain stores.

They held hands as they arrived back at their car which sat on the outer fringe of a parking lot at the mall. Alex smiled at Danielle as she slipped a final plastic bag into the trunk. Alex's trunk was already filled with plastic shopping bags of various sizes and colors as well as a paper grocery bag full of romance novels his wife intended to drop off at the local thrift store.

"I think you keep the bookshelf at the thrift store stocked single-handedly," Alex said, pointing to the paper bag.

"My brother's wife keeps sending them to me. And I never even read them. Maybe I should have sent her directions to the local thrift store in their Christmas card this year. Or would that have been tacky?"

"You could always re-gift them to another relative."

"Alex, I love my family."

Alex looked on at the boxed-up baby crib next to the bag of books. His heart grew heavy as he stared on at it. He noticed Danielle staring at it, too.

"Shall we do it?" She said, referring to the crib.

"I guess. I suppose we've talked about it enough."

"You don't sound sure."

He sighed. "I'm sure."

"Are you sure you're sure?"

"Sure I'm sure."

He slammed the trunk shut. She held out her hand so Alex could hand her the car keys. He dropped them into her gloved hand and admired her a moment. She stood there in a black, full-length winter coat with a white pair of earmuffs and ruddy cheeks. There was an unspoken melancholy in her eyes and he hated that.

He wandered over to the passenger side door and waited. Halfway to the driver's side door, Danielle stopped and held her stomach.

"Ugh. Maybe you should drive," she said.

"Bad pizza?"

"Maybe."

Alex circled the car and climbed into the driver's seat. Danielle climbed into passenger seat slowly as if she were carrying a baby.

"I'll start driving to the thrift store," said Alex. "But if you think you're going to be ill, tell me and I'll pull over."

"Okay."

He started the car and pulled out of the parking lot. It took great patience on his part to work his way through the maze of snow banks, illegally-parked cars, and people sitting in their cars waiting for a parking spot near the doors of the mall. He maneuvered his way to the exit and worked his way through the traffic like a seasoned professional. After all, he knew that if you did not get into the right lane at the right time, nobody would cut him any slack in traffic.

A few hundred feet later, they found themselves caught up in a snarl of traffic that seemed stretch around every street corner. It took minutes to move a block. Across the street was another set of stores collectively known as Ridge Square South, and Alex squinted as he tried to read the letters being installed over a new store taking up residence there.

"Check it out," he motioned to Danielle, pointing across the street. "Maybe it's a second store." There, a small crane put the last bright red letter into place to complete the phrase: "Erin's Books".

"Alex, maybe next time you can find a job in a field that is not so…I dunno…*involved.*"

"I'll try."

"And ask more questions before you take on any new projects."

Alex laughed.

"I'm serious."

"You being serious? That's a twist."

She put a hand to her stomach again, and closed her eyes a moment. She took a deep breath. "And don't go running off to stop riots either."

"I'll think about it."

"You always say that."

Alex drove on, eventually entering the freeway. Again, though, all he ended up doing was speeding up only to come to a crawl. He watched the other cars passing by and changing lanes in front of them like a chess game in slow motion. To Alex it seemed like a calculated waste of effort.

He glanced over at Danielle, who began to look pale now. "Are you going to make it?"

"I think so. Maybe we should go home and skip the thrift store."

"You sure?"

She glared back at him. "I'm sure I'm sure."

"Still think it was the pizza?"

She let out a loud sigh. "I don't know. You had the same kind. Are you feeling sick?"

"Nope. I'm ready for dessert. I'm thinking apple pie with ice cream."

She glared at him again and reclined the passenger seat.

Alex smiled. "Bad choice of words. Maybe we should head straight home."

A few miles later Alex passed by a billboard that used to advertise Aspirizon Bank. The ad was now replaced with an ad for a resort up north. "Looks like the bank lost their billboard."

Danielle remained silent for a minute, still watching the road, and still resting with the passenger seat leaning all the way back.

"It's a mystery, isn't it?" She said suddenly.

"What?"

"Answered prayers."

"What made you think of that?"

"I dunno. Sometimes I think I'm getting a 'no' for an answer, but then the answer arrives when I'm not even looking for it."

"What do you mean?"

"I didn't tell you this, but on that day I took David to the dentist, I felt the urge to pray for your safety. Several times."

"And?"

"I did. But I didn't want to at first. You made me mad."

Alex smiled. "I was safe. So you got your answers. I guess I could learn a thing or two about persistence in prayer from you."

"You're just realizing this now?"

He looked over to see her with her eyes closed, but with a sly smirk on her face. "It's amazing how God keeps track of it all, though, isn't it?"

* * *

Later that night in Maplewood, Kay and Brian sat in front of Brian's computer in his bedroom. The computer sat on a wooden desk across from his bed and next to a bookcase whose shelves sagged under the weight of two-inch thick programming manuals. To Kay, they looked like different-colored bricks that would not hold her interest for more than a page.

Next to her on the blue-speckled carpet were her beloved storyboards, done up in colored pencil and ink pen. She held one of them up and compared it to the game animation Brian brought up onscreen. She then wondered where he went wrong. After a moment, she set the storyboard back down and picked up a compact disc out of a cardboard box full of them. She turned it over in her hands and then watched Brian type out a few commands at the keyboard.

Brian looked back at the box and then up at her. "How many copies do you think we've moved over the past two weeks?" He asked.

She counted off the discs in the box and then counted the three remaining boxes on the floor. "Out of the box of two hundred you gave me, I think I have seventy-five left."

"That's awesome."

"How many do you think we'll move online tonight?"

"No idea. The forums are going crazy waiting for this upload. And I'm not about to let our adoring fans down."

Kay glanced over at another desk in her brother's room, which had a small sound mixing board and a microphone on a stand. "Did you podcast it?"

"Yep. I've been pitching it for weeks."

Brian looked up at a LAMPS poster on the wall and then at the clock. It was a few seconds before midnight. He held his finger over the enter key on the keyboard. As the second hand ticked to midnight even, he pressed the button.

At that, his computer began to upload the finished version of their first adventure game.

He leaned back in his wooden chair and put his hands behind his head. "Now the real fun begins."

Chapter Thirty-Five

The pile of puzzle pieces on the card table dwindled as Alex continued to plug them into the puzzle. With the sky complete, the rocks along the bottom edge all in place, the only thing left was a handful of pieces for the black and gray humpback whales surfacing in the middle of the picture.

The aroma of pumpkin pies baking in the oven teased him now as he downed a mug of nutmeg-topped eggnog. His wife spent the better part of this Christmas Eve morning baking cookies and pies in the kitchen and the results were now sitting on the counter. Every so often, he noticed one more cookie missing, and of course, David seemed clueless as to its whereabouts.

As he leaned back in his chair a moment, the cordless phone next to him rang. He picked it up. "Hello?"

"Hello, is this Alex?"

"This is."

"Hey, it's Drew. How are you? Have you been able to find any work yet?"

"I'm doing alright. As far as work—nothing yet."

"Okay. I've been checking around a few different places and I have a few friends over at a place in Eagan. They're hiring engineers right now. You interested?"

"Definitely."

"Okay. The company is Weinberger and Wheaton. I'll e-mail you all the contact info."

"Great. Thanks. How are you by the way?"

"Doing alright, Alex. Doing alright. I've got savings and several other ideas brewing. You know me, always something going on the back burner. But, like Lombardi said, 'it's not whether you get knocked down, it's whether you get up'."

"Great."

"Say, I wanted to update you on something. Remember what I told you about the fire? The detectives think they caught the kid that did it."

Alex leaned forward and listened intently. "Any idea who it was?"

"Some kid named Ben Travers. They caught him in Wisconsin with a bag of lighters and some empty bottles in his car. Eventually he confessed to a few things. Then they found a warehouse full of firebomb materials in Bloomington."

Alex's eyes widened. He ran a hand through his hair, but said nothing.

"You okay?"

"Sorry, just thinking. That's great, Drew. Glad they found him."

"Lucky I didn't get a hold of him. But I'll let you go. It's Christmas Eve. Enjoy your holiday."

They said their goodbyes and hung up. Alex had a difficult time containing his enthusiasm. When he got up, he found Danielle in the bathroom with the door closed.

He then stopped by the den to see David in front of the computer, swinging his legs and staring at the screen.

David held out a compact disc to his father. "Can you put this in? Pleeease?"

Alex stared on at the disc, which looked to be a version of Brian's game with modified cover art. His eyes widened. "Where'd you get this?"

"Mom got it. She said I could have it. Pleeease?"

"Where'd she get it?"

"At a bookstore."

David grinned big.

Alex walked over to the computer. He dropped the disc into the computer's disc tray and shut the door. His heart rate began to pick up as he watched the installation dialog box pop up on the screen. He read each line of the license agreement before clicking the "accept" button.

After it installed he continued to stare at the screen. David, however, looked like he was ready to play.

"Can I see something buddy?" He told his son.

"Ohhhkay."

David dove off the chair and pretended to fall to the floor. Alex took over his chair and launched the game. He scrutinized every scene, picked apart every line of spoken dialogue, and monitored every animation. He then shut the game down and launched it over and over again. There did not seem to be any sign of the "mark" message like before.

He heard a loud sigh behind him as David rolled around on the floor. He turned around to see David putting his hands over his eyes.

"Oh no. Now you've done it. Mom!"

David sprang up and ran off into the living room flailing his arms.

Alex shook his head and walked into the hallway where David met him head on. "It's all yours, bud."

He watched Danielle open the bathroom door and stare at him. She motioned for him to head into the bedroom. He could see she was holding something in her hands the entire time, however.

"What's going on?" He said, crossing his arms.

"Who called?"

"Drew. Sounds like he found an opportunity for me."

"A job?"

"Yes."

She grinned wide, but Alex could see something major was on her mind. He had not seen that look in her eyes since…

"Close your eyes," she directed. "And hold out your hand."

Alex closed his eyes and held out his hands. He figured he was setting himself up for a certain gag as she placed something in his hand. The object was made of plastic and for a moment he figured it was the digital thermometer from the medicine cabinet.

Then he opened his eyes. "You're pregnant?"

She grinned even bigger and held him tight.

Then came a shout from the den. "Dad! Look!"

Alex felt his heart rate pick up again as he raced into the bedroom. He half expected something to be destroying his hard drive or messages flashing across the screen. Instead he found David pointing eagerly at the screen and rocking back and forth on the chair. Alex stood behind his son's chair and watched a cute animation of a spacecraft zipping around the screen.

He then knelt down next to his son and watched for several minutes as the game progressed. The artwork was impressive, the animation fluid, and he hoped in the long run that his son got something out of it.

Alex smiled. "I beta tested that, you know."

About the Author

Michael Galloway is an outdoors enthusiast whose interests include camping, fishing, hiking, writing, and technology. He has a degree in Journalism, and has been writing software in one language or another for over forty years. He currently lives in Minnesota with his family.

* * *

Also by Michael Galloway

An Echo Through the Trees
Horizons
Gathering the Wind
Corridors
Fractal Standard Time
Ionotatron
Chronopticus Rising
The Chronopticus Chronicles
Race the Sky
The Hammer of Amalynth
Windows Out
The Fire and the Anvil
Gathering the Artists
Gathering the Swarm
Gathering the Hours
Flyover Country